CW00706743

Voracious

MAŁGORZATA LEBDA

Translated from the Polish
by Antonia Lloyd-Jones

Linden Editions

Linden Editions, 110 Standen Rd, London SW18 5TS
www.lindeneditions.com

This English-language edition published in the UK in 2025 by Linden Editions

First published by Społeczny Instytut Wydawniczy Znak, Sp. z o. o., Kraków, Poland, in 2023 with the title *Łakome*

9 8 7 6 5 4 3 2 1

ISBN: 978-1-0687404-0-4
eISBN: 978-1-0687404-1-1

A CIP catalogue record for this book is available from the British Library.

Cover image © Maria Nurek
Cover design © Tasja Puławska

Text design and typesetting by Tetragon, London
Printed in England by TJ Books Limited, Padstow, Cornwall

This publication has been supported by the ©POLAND Translation Programme.

EU Authorised Representative: Easy Access System Europe – Mustamäe tee 50, 10621 Tallinn, Estonia, gpsr.requests@easproject.com.

To loss.

And also the birds.

Voracious

WILD CHERRY

Danube's howling. And they're here already, just as I remember them – hungry, busy. They're shining as if their wings were coated in petrol, shimmering violet, blue, red and yellow.

The flock is hovering above the village.

June has absorbed a lot of sunlight, and at this early stage the fruit of the wild cherry trees is already sweet.

Grandpa, who avoids Grandma's illness, and to whom any ceremony around illness is alien, the man who refuses to know anything about illness, or to touch anything that's ill, stands on the veranda, watching the way the starlings are lowering their flight above the orchard.

He bangs a metal bar against an aluminium milk churn. The sound rumbles around the valley.

And I'm watching him. It must be rumbling inside him too, his body's shaking, he has skin like the skin of the men who inhabit the Carpathian Arch, I think. Bronze. Ebony.

The starlings take off – there's a vast horde of them. As they fly over the house, they cast a shadow on the floor of the west room, the one that in chilly months is heated by a cast-iron stove.

In a while they're back above the orchard.

They're persistent.

More banging against metal sends them into nervous jitters. The rumbling keeps them in flight.

Grandpa has a cigarette break. They take advantage of the silence to land on a spreading tree. They stuff their small bodies with fruit.

They've learnt to recognize silence, I say to Ann.

Yes, she agrees.

Ann is the brightness here. She's interested in the light, and she is the light. She came here this morning from a distant country, straight to this warm village known as May. She still has the journey in her. She still has a smell that's not from here – freesia, patchouli. She's with me on the veranda, letting her sight adjust to early summer.

Her eyes follow the light.

Ann knows about the light.

She studies the light.

She hunts the light.

She can tell the future from the light.

I touch her neckline, where there are constellations of moles.

You should count them, says Ann.

All right, I reply.

In childhood I used to count Grandma's birthmarks. She didn't hide much from me. She let me count the dots that covered her back, as well as the ones around her breasts. She let my gaze into nooks and crannies such as her ear canal or the crook of her elbow.

You come from my body too, she'd say.

We move from the veranda into the west room. We can hear Grandpa playing his tune. Grandma is watching the shadow of the flock of birds. She raises an emaciated hand, as if offering to answer in class.

There, she says, pointing at the wardrobe.

She asks me to fetch out her summer dresses. I'm surprised. Usually she wears the pyjamas I buy for her at the market in Stary Sad, the nearby town. She likes the ones the colour of powdered mint.

I lay out the dresses on the sofa bed.

This one, whispers Grandma.

She has chosen a dress the colour of blood. I pick it up. It's velvet.

Take it to him, she says.

I do it without a word of protest.

On the veranda, Grandpa is finishing another 'Klub', as he calls any cigarette out of sentiment for the brand he smoked in the past, a habit I've inherited from him. He takes hold of the dress. His cuticle catches on the material. He sniffs the fabric.

Róża, he says.

I'm looking at him. The last few years have withered his body. More and more often he looks away, avoids eye contact, glances aside. He can't hold and return my gaze. I'd like to see him stronger, I think to myself.

He turns around and says: Come with me.

I follow him.

He heads towards his workshop.

On the spot he knocks some pieces of hazel wood together in the shape of a rough cross, and then clothes it in Grandma's blood-red dress. He inspects his handiwork. He adjusts the foam pads, which give the object a surprised expression, as if something alive were raising its shoulders.

Will it do? he asks.

Yes, I reply.

I know he needs me to say yes. Here, in this illness, there's no room for objection.

Grandpa says yes to my yes. He picks up the dress-clad skeleton and carries it into the orchard. There's a procession behind him: Danube the dog and Azrael the tomcat.

Grandma is watching us from the window of the west room. She's scratching the skin on her cheek. I know that reflex. It appears whenever she's staring at something. She's capable of scratching herself all over without being aware of it.

Grandpa sets a ladder to the trunk of a cherry tree. I assist. He cautiously places his feet on the rungs. He reaches the top. He ties the bird scarer to the branches with wire.

Starvation stopper, more like, I mutter to myself.

Grandma's red dress starts to move in the wind. A gust enters it and fills the void where her warm body used to be. It looks as if the dress has come alive.

The spirit of the orchard, I say to Ann, as she joins us.

Nothing works as well as a bright red dress, she croons the words of a Polish rap song.

The starlings are circling above the tree.

Back in the west room I ask Grandma if she can remember wearing that frock last spring. There are photos to prove it.

She says yes.

The red emphasized her white hair.

You know what, she says, the illness must have been in me by then already. Can you imagine?

Yes, I say.

My fingertips inspect the wound she has scratched on her cheek.

For the rest of the day we take turns to go up to the window of the west room and look into the orchard. The blood-red of the dress blends with the cherries ripening in the full sun. We'll pick the fruit we've saved from the starling beaks for Grandma. Grandpa will make them into sweet jam.

THE WEST ROOM

We're refreshing the room on the west side of the house for the illness. For years on end in my childhood it served as a capacious cold store. This is where we used to stow the meat of pigs killed to mark church feasts. And my grandparents kept furniture in here, old paintings, jars filled with preserves, churns full of honeydew honey and cardboard boxes packed with Christmas decorations. Since the tragedy, the one that befell my parents and my aunt many years ago, this has been Grandma's winter lair.

Soon the radiator ribs will be installed in here, says Grandpa, standing on the threshold of the room.

Yes, I say.

Grandma mustn't freeze while she's ill, he says.

Yes, yes, I say.

I can still put up with the cold, says Grandma, but get the pink out of here.

Yes, yes, I say.

The pink reminds me of meat, she says.

Yes, I say.

Make it white in here, please.

I say yes.

I am obedient, this is why I've come back from far away, this is why I left my life in a place that's always bright, so as to be obedient.

Obedience, I say to Ann.

Obedience, she repeats, and passes a hand over my hair.

DEAL

We start to refresh the room. As if the illness were demanding special measures and actions of us.

We're cooperating, I think to myself, we're doing a deal with it.

It's got us as well now, I say to Ann, as I hand her the dungarees I used to wear here in my teens.

We work in tandem. The illness unites us in physical labour. We need to wear ourselves out.

Grandma's eyes are vigilant.

Grandma's eyes follow us, watching and watching.

Let's work ourselves to death, I say.

Now and then Grandma peeps into the room and nods, watching and watching. She's pleased that the plants and holy pictures will stand out against the white walls.

Make it white in here, she asks again.

The guidelines are simple – white.

We strip off old layers of paint with the help of a putty knife. We hand each other tools at moments when our labouring shoulders and arms begin to ache. I can taste dust on my lips, and it's grating between my teeth.

I'm holding the ladder on which Ann is standing. She's at grips with the wall. Her arms are bare, and there's fine dust settling on them. I can see her muscles working. She's beautiful as she wields the putty knife. She's removing layers of paint that have accumulated over the past thirty years. There's a lot to be read from them. They contain a record of the festive occasions that demanded redecoration of the room: christening, first communion, confirmation, and now illness. I recognize each of the colours that comes off.

Maybe by studying them one could read more in them, just as one can read changes in the environment from a section of soil.

The history of this house is falling to the floor.

We're making space for a new story.

Ann is beautiful as she tenses her body and activates her thoughts, as she talks, and as everything that she is gets moving.

We need the brightness, I tell her as I mix the paint.

Yes, she says.

We're both covered in white stains.

At night, as the room dries, I enter it to examine the interior.

Whoooo, hooo, I hoot.

I can hear Ann behind me.

Whoooo, hooo, she repeats after me.

The noises vibrate within these dozen square metres.

We're hawking from the dust. We've got it in our windpipes. We're spitting white.

Next morning we show Grandma the room.

It's white, she says.

She puts her cool hands to our faces and strokes us, just as she strokes Danube whenever he comes home after days out gallivanting.

Grandma starts carrying houseplants into the west room.

Life, life, she says.

After two pots of prayer plants she weakens. She sits on the floor and leans against the wall. Without a word we take on her work, we become her hands. We carry the plants that were left in the hall during the renovation into the west room: aloe, asparagus, fern, geranium, Siberian ivy, Christmas cactus, philodendron, croton, dracaena, begonia, elephant's ears.

Grandma's eyes are vigilant.

Grandma's eyes follow us.

Grandma's eyes are watching, watching.

CRESCENT

Once the smell of paint has gone, we spend the night in the west room, the three of us. We don't yet know that it will stay this way, that we're going to spend night after night together. But that's not yet now. Now the moon is waxing.

There it is, waxing crescent, I think to myself.

I'm getting used to closeness.

Between us we share a bed and a sofa bed.

We remove our daytime layers of clothing.

We mingle our odours.

My women are beautiful, I think as I fall asleep, and they're fragrant, fragrant.

THROAT

In the room I can hear Grandma and Ann breathing. Night has brought our restive daytime pupils to a stop. Ever since the illness came to live with us, I've been the last to fall asleep.

I'm the only strong sentry, I think to myself. No one else can stay on guard for as long as I can.

In a corner of the room the cast-iron stove releases warmth. The final days in June have brought a chill here, to the valley.

It's just about to start.

The light.

The light bisects our faces. I'm looking at Ann, whose features are lit by the headlamps of a truck carrying cattle to the slaughterhouse. She opens her eyes. And hers are deep, bottomless. They examine the waking world, and when they notice me looking, they stop.

For a while Ann keeps watch with me.

But she can't remain on guard as well as I can.

She falls asleep.

Here we are, it's starting. A few dozen metres from the west room large trucks are turning the bend, and their headlamps flood the interior with light.

Bright and dark.

Bright and dark.

Bright.

Dark.

Bright.

It'll go on for a million years.

I have time, I tell myself.

The trucks are transporting animals to the slaughterhouse. I imagine the bodies of cows – warm and damp.

As a child I didn't always manage to stay awake until this point of the night. Sometimes I would drop off and be woken by the show once it had already started. It was accompanied by noises like today's: guttural, protracted sounds that instead of dissolving in space can hang over the village for ages.

Cows mooing.

Dogs whining.

The night hooting.

And that too – the smell: of dung, urine, sweat.

I can see the bodies of my women clearly as they're lit by the slow motion of the headlamps. Their features – depending on the falling light, and also the shadow – are now dead, now alive.

Grandma is lying on her side, with a hand under her left cheek. She looks like a child. A child of the kind they'd like to have from me.

But now is not the time for life. Death – that's what fills my head. I'm at its service. Grandma is my child. I am my grandmother's mother. And that's all right, I think.

Ann's body is close by. I'm endlessly amazed by the porcelain of her skin, the white of her hair, eyelashes and eyebrows. There's something identical in us and there's also – as we're aware – something in us that bonds us: plenty of the prodigal.

The bodies of my dearest women are reacting to the light, beneath their eyelids their eyeballs are in motion.

Just a little longer.

They open their eyes.

One after the other.

Grandma looks and whispers into the light: Water or fire will deal with it.

Woken up again, Ann sets her bare feet on the floorboards; her toenails are painted dark burgundy. As are mine. We paint them for ourselves, not for our people, who are far away now. They have to be far away, I won't let them come near the illness. I belong to the illness, not to them. There's only room for Ann here. She can plunge those painted toenails into dung or compost, she can splash around in it.

I think of us as sisters in whatever's decomposing.

Ann takes a packet of Klubs from the pocket of Grandpa's overcoat, which she has put on.

Come on, she says to me.

I wrap myself in a blanket and follow her. Grandma is watching the lights running across the ceiling.

Perhaps she's fallen asleep again, I think, but her watching is still awake. She's scariest when from her gaze you can't tell who her eyes belong to.

We go out onto the veranda. I can feel the cold.

The concert, I say to Ann.

She hands me a cigarette lit off hers.

It's starting, I say.

Yes, she says.

Aha, there it is.

We listen.

The hooves know no rhythm, I say.

After a while the animals start to sing.

They're singing, I say.

Ann puts a finger to my lips, trapping the cigarette smoke inside me.

The animals are singing. Their song comes from within, from their warm bellies, I think to myself.

After a while the dogs respond. First the Keeshond at Rybowicz's place below the bluff on the other side of the village, then the dogs at the slaughterhouse start exercising their throats, soon after that Danube joins in, followed by the parish chairwoman's Samoyeds and the dogs chained by their kennels at the presbytery, descendants of those frisky mongrels that have been interbreeding for generations along the village gullies. They have the names of the evangelists: Mark, John, Luke. There's also a black one that the village has christened Blackamoor.

How strange, I'm thinking, I can tell the howls apart, I recognize the tune of each different dog. Not much longer here and I'll be able to guess what each howl is for, what its purpose is.

Ann removes her finger from my lips.

You know what, I say, I've always wanted to be one of the village dogs, to have the whole of May as my own. To know no borders. I've felt tempted to be far from what's human. To have a canine body, and to act in harmony with it, to succumb to hunger, to refuse myself nothing. To fawn on only the chosen few, to nip and bark at everything else. To be a choosy bitch. To love just one person, to do my duty by them, to obey them. And also to disappear for days on end. To have the right to do that, and to take advantage of it.

Take advantage, repeats Ann.

The barking carries, setting off further noises.

The whole village is howling.

Tonight this place is like the deep throat of a hungry animal, I'm thinking.

FAITH

At night the slaughterhouse wakes the birds. This has consequences for the valley. Time gets muddled. Something within time slackens. People open their eyes at the wrong moment, and enter the day in a stupor. At noon they look at the sun, but where it stands in the sky doesn't seem right to them.

It confuses Grandpa very badly. Grandpa gets up with the birds. The brightness startles him.

I wake up and it's empty, he says, telling me about these instances.

Empty? I ask.

Empty, yes, there's nothing to grab hold of, there's nothing to give you your bearings, he says.

He gets up in the night and walks about the house. He climbs a ladder to the attic and paces in there. He strides to and fro, which calms him down. He also finds it soothing to stroke the antlers he's been collecting for several decades. When Grandpa confuses night and day he sometimes falls asleep up there.

In the mornings, when I go and take my place at the desk to work on code, pure, intuitive and beautiful, the kind I sometimes dream about, I often find him among the antlers. Grandpa has a story for each one. He invents lives for these bone tissues. To get him to tell one of these stories you have to go up to him and praise his collection in the attic. His tales about deer are full of the forest and animals in a panic, they take place in rain and fog. Only from that sort of weather do animals emerge in Grandpa's tales.

RIVERS

Waking the birds is a sin, says Grandma.

In the orchard belonging to the slaughterhouse nothing has been born for years. The earth there is trodden down by herds of cows. Most of the animals are unloaded at the top of the hill and led straight into concrete walls. The ones for whom there's no room in the cool stalls are let into the orchard. They take the opportunity to empty their deep bellies, pissing as if they had endless rivers inside them. Urine in such large quantities scorches the earth, so it's hard for the trees to grow here.

The orchard is bare, stunted and sick.

It's because of moisture from inside the cows, I say.

Fire or water will deal with it, says Grandma.

I believe her.

The greengage trees in the orchard haven't borne fruit for years, she says.

Yes, I say.

SWEET

Grandma can't resist any living thing. She'd take everything that's alive into the west room, she'd invite it in. Her wish is for living things to be there before her eyes, to be moving about, to make scratching and buzzing noises.

Let it strut around, she says.
  Let it flutter, she says.
  Let it be, she says.

Grandma has adored living things for ever, that's to say for as long as I can remember. I think one could track the generations of everything that has multiplied here, in the western part of the house. And if one were to ask the last of these generations, the living one, where they're from, then if they could talk, they'd be sure to say they were from the cool room of the human, the humaness, Róża.

Her wish, I think, is for living things to occupy her mind, especially now, to give rise to responsibilities, to divert her attention from the illness.

Grandma studies living things with curiosity. This passion, as I call it – this weakness, as Grandpa calls it – has rendered her useless so many times.

It was a nightmare, taking Róża to the field, Grandpa begins, reminding me at the same time of my childhood.

The moment Grandma saw a grasshopper in the scythed wheat, he says, she'd drop the work she was doing and pick it up. She'd cup her hands around the insect's body to construct a sealed home for it and carry it to the boundary strip. And there she'd talk to that living thing and set it down on a wild strawberry leaf, a wild garlic leaf, or some tiny yellow pimpernel leaves. And chase it away into the forest. Shoo, she'd cry after the insect, anything to keep it far from the harvest blades.

Then I'd follow her onto the boundary strip, watchfully, as if suspecting a holy rite was happening there. Grandma herself was a saint to me. In those days I'd give her all sorts of names. Like:

Saint Grandma Róża talking to insects.

Saint Grandma Róża the tender.

Saint Grandma Róża the just.

Saint Grandma Róża the compassionate.

Saint Grandma Róża the merciful.

Saint Grandma Róża who is.

For fuck's sake, Róża, Grandpa would shout, and Grandma would return to the field to go on sowing confusion and interrupting the work of human muscles and heated-up machines. For at once a new living thing would find its way into her hands.

Then, as Grandma walked towards the forest again, the rebellion in her would start its ritual too. She'd be defying Grandpa, his imprecations and curses. At such moments two forces would go head to head, two things that were sacred: the sanctity of work, and the sanctity of a tiny life. And as I can see now, years on, Grandma was also holding back time and controlling it in her own way.

On these occasions Grandpa would sit under one of the wild apple trees, take out some bread and some pork fat, and cut it into teeny little pieces. He'd chew it pensively, tell me to take some and chew it too. He wouldn't do any more swearing because his mouth would be occupied with something else.

And God forbid any larger living thing would be found in the mown grass or the ploughed field. Grandma would devote all the care she had – has – in her to the living thing. The worst, meaning the most wonderful, were moles. They stirred great pity in Grandma. She'd lament over them, poke a stick into a dug-up molehill in search of the entrance to their tunnel and stuff the male, female or baby mole into that hole in the ground.

Go home, go home, she'd cry to the mouldwarp life.

But later on, if she chanced to see one of these living things dead, she'd bury it in the earth and decorate the spot with stones. And now, as you walk about the fields of May, you can still happen upon this funerary land art created by Róża.

She'd be angry whenever Grandpa ploughed something living out of the earth and in the process it became dead. Every time she'd lose her voice. Years later I understood – she was upset. She wouldn't talk to anyone or anything. A night had to go by, sleep had to pour through Grandma, and then her speech returned.

Not at all long ago I mentioned this in a conversation with Grandpa. As he put it: Yes, Róża was upset, but it was hard to be angry or be upset with her, because she'd be angry so beautifully, splendidly.

Splendidly. No one pronounces the word 'splendidly' as splendidly as Grandpa, I thought at the time, and added it to my dictionary. And sometimes, in various situations, I say: Splendidly.

Nor did I ever see Grandma grazing the cows. As he betrayed to me, Grandpa had taken that duty away from her before my arrival in the world.

Large animals, he said, cause Róża total mental confusion.

Once he told me more about it: Everything to do with grazing the cows bewildered her, she felt sorry for the cattle, she talked to the cattle and wanted to set the animals free, to have a bit of life, as she put it. She even threatened to let them run wild if I went on tying their heads to their forelegs with chains. But how can you not tie them when they've always been tied? And once, when I'd chained their heads to their legs that way – so they couldn't raise those heads of theirs, as you know, so they couldn't trot off – then, pardon me, but Róża splendidly lost her fucking rag. She got down to business as soon as I disappeared from her view, but she hadn't disappeared from mine, because I was hiding in the shadows.

What did you see? I asked.

What did I see? She started tinkering with the chains. She pulled the toggles out of the rings. One after another the cows raised their heads. It looked as if they were raising them to gaze into the summer sky. Grandma stood in the middle of the herd, rested her hands against her sides and said: There now. As if on command the cows moved from the spot. Each in a different direction, as if they'd had enough of living in a herd. They spread about the village, they caused damage all over May. I know, because people brought those cows back to me from various corners of the village and they told me. One cow had darted off to our parish chairwoman; her father was still the chairman then; another had gone down towards the reservoir from the topmost fields; a third went off to the slaughterhouse and got among those cows in the orchard, the people there almost did her in, but they could see she was too clean for the knacker's and someone recognized her as ours; a fourth got into the priest's orchard and stuffed herself on windfalls; another one I found that night in the brook, with some plastic sticking from her mouth, she'd eaten an empty saltpetre bag; a sixth turned up three days later, she came out of a birch grove, stuffed with food and given a wash by the August downpours.

What did Róża say? I asked.

She found great joy in it, in their freedom.

TO THE WATERS

Grandma is uncompromising in her defence of living things, I think, but she does concede to death too. It happens whenever Grandpa raises a hand to a pigeon – only then does she not protest. She keeps watch over other lives, she guards other lives like her own.

If a big fat fly, the kind that has fed on the flesh of animals from the slaughterhouse, drunk its fill of the blood of animals from the slaughterhouse and touched the shit of animals from the slaughterhouse, if one of those creatures – Grandpa calls those huge insects that shine against the light 'dung flies' – flies into Grandma's room, it will now be safe in that room for life. For years I've called it the bluebottle rest home.

Nothing in Grandma's room could be killed – and this rule remains in force – nothing living can be removed from there. Up to a point. Before painting the interior Ann and I had to perform an evacuation, a solemn removal from the room.

Grandma was present, keeping watch, pointing with her index finger: Here and here, and here too, and there, behind the picture, behind the wardrobe, in the crack between the boards.

The lives of many household tenants passed through the jars we were holding: lots of spiders of the Pholcidae family; and lots and lots of harvestmen.

Every living thing remained alive.

And now life is returning. It may be the same spiders spinning their threads and constructing their webs. In Grandma's room they have truly spa-like conditions. I imagine that just as one says, 'I'm off to the waters,' which means to me that a person is going away for a rest, so the insects communicate with each other, saying, 'I'm off to Róża's.'

But it's not enough for Grandma. She wants more living things in her room. That may be why she needs both of us here too, me and Ann, so there's something moving, breathing, stirring, exuding warmth.

In the other part of the house, where Grandpa holds office, matters are completely different. Anything that's alive but not human dies on the spot, it doesn't multiply, it doesn't take up space, and it doesn't buzz.

In the warm months Grandpa carries a green fly swat about the house under his arm, one of the pear-shaped kind. And with this pear he inflicts death. Twice a day he sweeps out the kitchen and the east room. When the bristles of the broom working in his hands come close to the hot stove, the whole force of Grandpa's tidiness lands on the dustpan that's waiting there: the tiny bodies of insects mixed with dust, hair and table crumbs. Grandpa bends over, opens the door under the hob wide, and with an abrupt gesture, to save his hand from the flames, he flicks off the tiny bodies of the dead things that used to be living.

Grandma cannot bear it.

I can't bear it, she says.

Then she closes her eyes, like a child who has seen a parent weeping, or the nakedness of something that it shouldn't see naked. And won't open them until she hears: Done.

It's usually me that says 'done'.

For me, the worst things are the sound of burning and the smell of hair thrown into the fire. After this holocaust Grandpa straightens up and goes onto the veranda to smoke a Klub. I call this his tidying cigarette. Before lighting the tidying cigarette he says: All tidy, there.

But Grandma rewards the living things that are in the house by transferring them into the whiteness of the west room. Whenever she sees a spider in the kitchen, she catches it in a glass tumbler or a jar and takes it to her room; if she sees a stray butterfly she might catch it in her hands and transfer it there. I once saw her trying to chase out a large, fat dung fly, well fed on animals from the slaughterhouse, from one part of the house to the other. At the time I imagined that Grandma could specialize in this chasing, that she could be like a shepherd dog, a Border collie for example, and that she'd know how to herd flies just as it herds sheep.

Madness, I once called all these efforts of Grandma's. I said it straight to her face after spending the whole morning transferring harlequin ladybirds for her, from the kitchen to the corner of her room. But when I saw that tears were welling in her eyes because of my words, to stop those tears I said: I'm sorry.

She needed to feel that she had me, that she could squeeze me and have more of me.

I have to be helped with this, she pushed past the lump in her throat.

Yes, I said, because I'd remembered that here, now, in these circumstances it was necessary to say yes.

Yes, the word rumbled inside me, because it alone was good and right here and now.

'Yes,' I wrote with a fingernail on the palm of my hand, I wrote it so that it hurt, so I wouldn't forget.

Yes, I said.

No, I thought.

That's how I became complicit in Grandma's madness. And although I'm afraid, it's usually my job to smuggle in moths for her, the ones with the death's head on their backs and those white ones speckled with little black spots. All this I offer up, like a sacrifice, in her room.

Grandma reacts to each of these moths as if the cow had just calved, that favourite cow of hers, Malina, as if the calf, a bullock, were already standing on his own legs, licked clean of slime, healthy and handsome, had put his head beneath the udder and were sucking, butting his hard brow against his mother's warm teats. I'm familiar with Grandma's joy, the motion of her wrinkles and the quiver of her lips that accompany both moths and cows.

At night she's pleased when I switch on the bedside lamp that's protected by wire netting and the moths fly down to that light, but also to her, to Grandma.

They're dancing for us, she says on those occasions.

It's impossible to disagree with her.

MUSIC

Here in the village of May we can never forget about the winter. We must sow, weed and water, so that in autumn we can reap a sufficient harvest.

As soon as the Ice Saints have gone by, when the month of May tips towards its second half, the planting here grows bolder. Now, as faith would have it, the frost can't get in here.

Thinking about the winter has force, it topples sturdy ash trees on the boundary strips, it eats away at the woods and birch groves.

The men of this village are afraid of the winter. The men of this place have been cursing the winter since time began. The men of this valley get firewood ready for the cold, planning to chase away the frosts with it.

Straight after the winter, when the woodsheds are still full of logs, the table saws start up. From dawn to dusk on working days music is played here on timber. The instruments are operated by the hands of men and women. I can recognize the strokes and rhythm of some of those playing.

And there are plenty of players: Grandpa, whose music resonates calm and a subtle main theme; Rybowicz, in whose playing a sort of out-of-tune string can be heard, like putting one's tongue to an exposed nerve in a tooth; the parish chairwoman, whose sawing has a rhythm, as if she cut everything to a military tune; the young Swart boys, brothers of the older Swarts – when I hear the music of their machine I fear for my fingers, they can also bend the sounds, there's nothing calm about this cutting, there's tension, a whistle; and finally the priest at the presbytery, whose table saw emits a noise like the buzzing of a mosquito.

The music of the table saws is the most beautiful, I think. Added to it are the sounds of the chainsaws, but that's the same everywhere, like a support band for a heavy metal group.

The people of May are afraid of the winter and the cold.

The music of machines reduces their fear.

The music of machines upsets the birds. Now, in June, it rings out non-stop. The white wagtails, jays and yellowhammers raise their voices at the rare moments when the hands of the people working the machines reach for cigarettes or water, or wipe the sweat from their brows, and then the birdsong pushes its way through the valley.

THE SILK ROUTE

Grandma contrives ways to have more living things in her room. Like today, when the sun is leading me, Ann and Grandpa into the fresh air. Grandma wants to stay in the kitchen. Alone. That should be enough to stir my suspicions. She has never avoided the light, she has never refused to go outside. She has always been drawn to the earth, she has found urgent, essential tasks that take the spine low, close to the soil, close to living things.

My vigilance has been put to sleep, I admit, by a thirst for the warmth of July.

Grandma asks us to make her tea before we go out, and to pass her a jar of last year's honeydew honey.

Ann drenches a tailed teabag.

I'm struggling with the jar. It's sealed tight. I prise the lid up with a knife. I unscrew it and hand the jar to Grandma.

We leave the house.

Outside we're stopped by the strawberry patches. I planted lots of varieties here in the spring: Elkat, Kama, Polka. The weeds have clasped the bushes in their embrace and are strangling them, they really are! I recognize shepherd's purse, knotgrass, and a profusion of dead-nettles. I lean over the first weed to hand and know at once I'll be spending the next few hours bowing to the ground. Ann lowers her body in the wake of mine. She's not dressed for work of this kind, everything she's wearing is white, of a shade that isn't seen here, in the countryside. There's no such thing in nature.

It's another element of her research into light, it occurs to me.

She's shining in the summer greenery.

Songbirds fill the air with sound.

Grandpa is setting wax foundations into new hive frames.

Nobody says anything to anyone.

And that's good.

Fingers plunging in the earth calm everything that's trembling inside me.

On our return to the house the silence worries us. Grandma doesn't respond to our calls. She must have gone back to her room.

Here in the warmth she's missing, I think, as if I were starting a new poem that, I'm also thinking, I won't be able to continue.

As I cross the kitchen threshold, Ann grabs me by the arm.

Look, she whispers, and nods at the floor.

I stop, and immobilize my raised foot, which was just about to land on the threshold to complete my step.

I look.

Grandma has marked out a honeyed trail. The silk route of this house. All, as one might have expected, for the ants.

Grandpa told me long ago that underneath the house there is not one, but several ant kingdoms. Ever since, I've been trying to imagine these underground worlds. I find this insect architecture inconceivable.

It's not the same as for bees, ants have lots of queen mothers, he said, and inside me my imagination built a series of underground floors for the anthill.

Forever, meaning as far back as I can remember, Grandma has been waging war against Grandpa over the ants. These conflicts start up in early spring. Major arguments, the subject of which is the petty little life of ants. But Grandma has never taken this life so literally into her own hands.

Every year in March the ants travel to the surface along numerous little tunnels. They colonize the kitchen, in particular. They get onto the shelves, form busy layers on any knife that's rashly left on the table after spreading a slice of bread with jam, and they infiltrate cans of honey. They can scent out sweetness. This species, our local kind, is very fond of fruit drops, and they settle in the pockets of Grandpa's clothes, because Grandpa happens to share this predilection with them.

Year after year Grandpa follows their trail, trying – as he puts it – to purge the terrain. He scatters the ant channels with toxic substances, sprays them with caustic concoctions and reaches for – as he puts it – the heavy chemicals. On these occasions Grandma wrings her hands.

You're a monster, she says.

You're a torturer, she says.

You're a vagabond, she says.

You're a butcher, she says.

He bristles most of all at the word 'butcher', that hurts him, that can put a stop to his task of inflicting death.

They'll devour us, they'll gnaw us to the bone, he replies to her on these occasions.

He never carries the victory. After a few days' silence the ants return. They're brought back to life despite the heavy chemicals.

Today Grandma has taken advantage of our absence, and in the exact spot where the insects emerge from their underground kingdom, or several kingdoms, right by the side of the chest of drawers, she has dripped some tea that's sweet with honey. She has carried the line on, across the floorboards in the kitchen and the hall, thus guiding an endless stream of ants into her room.

We walk along, Ann and I, with our spines bent over the floor as we observe the profusion of living things. I half open the bedroom door and I can see Grandma. There she sits, wearing Grandpa's glasses and leaning over the bedside cabinet. She has set down a plate, and on it a spoon, into which she has poured tea.

She's watching the living things, the traffic of living things.

After a while, as if she knows we're staring at her, she says: Nothing will come of it, they're going back in there – she nods towards the kitchen. To their death.

And indeed, when I look more closely, I notice that we're dealing with two moving lines: one runs towards the bedside cabinet, and the other, probably sated by now, is going back to the underground kingdom.

Will they come out alive? The kitchen is terrain where Grandpa is on guard. Monster. Torturer. Vagabond. Butcher.

Grandma touches the plate and examines the way the ants settle on her hand. Gazing from the dish are the eyes of Our Lady of Częstochowa. The insects' legs are sticky, which slows down their movements, and they're losing strength.

Break the line, says Grandma in a tone as if issuing an order.

I obediently wipe a stretch of the honey-sprinkled floor. After a moment of disorientation the ants divide into two camps. One lot goes towards the kitchen, and then down, towards the anthill, in order – so I imagine – to use their feelers to transmit the news to other feelers that the trail has been broken. The others set off towards the bedside cabinet. There, paddling in sweetness, they gradually cool their activity.

As I watch this I'm thinking: There she is, Grandma, part of the force that, in eternally desiring good, sometimes does harm.

THE EARTH

The earth is moving.

So there's water, says Grandma.

We look. The soil holding up the heavy slaughterhouse buildings is working away.

After several warm July days, heavy rains followed. The moisture has disturbed structures, entering deep enough to touch the stony inside of the hill.

The moisture has made itself at home in there, the moisture has its den in there, where it's burrowing, I say.

Yes, say Grandma and Ann in agreement.

The animals have been released from the slaughterhouse into the orchard. The procedures involving their bodies have been halted. Villagers are coming down the hill in cars and parking by the ditches along the main road. It's like the crowd on the feast day of our parish patron, Saint Roch.

From the veranda I'm watching the men's nervous activities. Grandpa is among them. He's looking and listening.

He'll bring home a story, I'm thinking.

When he comes back, all he says is: The earth is taking revenge.

That night, unlike in recent days, the slaughterhouse doesn't wheeze. No heavy vehicles come around the bend. Nothing lights up the room or the faces of my women.

The animals have gone quiet, they're spending the night on the damp earth of the stunted orchard.

I wake Ann.

Come on, I say.

Over my vest I throw on an anorak that belongs to Grandma, and Ann puts on Grandpa's waistcoat. We smell of them. I smell of a mixture of rye, sourdough, wild rosehips crushed in one's fingers, lard rubbed on one's hands, and ash removed from the ash pan. I put my nose to Ann and sniff. She smells of the stable and the earth, and also smoke from the rotting alder wood that Grandpa uses to smoke out the bees.

We walk up to the boundary strip to look at the bodies of the large animals. I want to remember what their muzzles are like. In the orchard, above the cast-iron bathtub that serves as a water trough, there's a lamp sizzling. Moths and mosquitoes are swirling around it. The cows' large muzzles are mashing fodder.

The animals seem dazed by the smells and sounds of the nearby forest, I'm thinking.

Amid the herd destined for meat we notice the fireflies of headlamps. Two men from the slaughterhouse are on watch beside them. They're like dogs. They're not talking to each other, as if afraid they'll wake something. The shafts of light from their headlamps run along the boundary strip from where we're spying on them. We're hidden from their view by a stout ash tree.

We watch.

When Ann's lips go blue with cold, I say: Come on.

Ann forms her lips into a spout and replies: Whoooohooo, whoooohooo.

The men raise their heads.

The men crane their necks.

They look like alarmed meerkats, whispers Ann.

Yes, I say.

The shafts of light turn first to the sky, as if they were sure the hooting came from there. Then they comb the forest with them and come close to the thicket on the boundary line. Ann would look at those lights endlessly, so I catch her by the hand. Our fingers intertwine. I pull Ann to the ground. We squat, and like that we retreat towards the house. Our calves and thighs are burning.

In the room, without a word we lie down on the sofa bed, one part of which is a tad higher than the other. Each night we swap places – one of us sleeps by the wall, the other facing the room.

I hug Ann, her back fits me perfectly. She bends her legs. And I bend mine. We fit our bodies together. I bring my lips close to her ear and whisper: Whoooohooo, whoooohooo.

HUSH

For a week there's been silence in the village. The downpour never stops. The table saws have been dragged into the sheds. The slaughterhouse makes no noise. Cracks are appearing in the concrete buildings. The earth continues to move.

It's quiet.

Hush.

Grandpa doesn't know what to do with himself. I can see he'd like to occupy his hands with something, or occupy his head with something.

At night, when I send a litany of code across the ocean via the internet, I can hear him climbing the stairs to the attic.

He notices me.

May I? he asks, and nods at the collection of antlers.

Of course, I say over my shoulder.

He walks to and fro among the antlers like the lord of the manor. Here he'll touch, there he'll adjust so they hang in a straight line. He occupies his hands with the coarse cast-offs that grew from the heads of mammals that inhabit the nearby forest. I set aside my work. I watch Grandpa.

There's so much quiet in him, I think. How can one hear what's inside him?

I go up to the biggest rack of antlers hanging from the roof.

Beautiful, I say.

Yes, he says.

He opens his mouth.

I found it in a clearing in the middle of the forest, he says, the one by the topmost fields. I was led there on a path trodden by animals. First I saw the right cast-off. When you see shed antlers, a sort of something appears inside you that occupies your mind for a long time. Something seems to come into being and enter your bloodstream. Then your senses are sharpened. You search for the rest. So I searched. And I found. In the middle of the clearing was the left cast-off. I counted, left and right, it was a beautiful rack with ten tines on each antler. I tossed them on my back and for a while in that clearing I was like an animal. A strange feeling. Mist was emerging from the forest, wreathing around me. Now and then something crackled in the brushwood. I imagined I was the animal. I froze – as alert as a buck that has scented hunters. Perhaps that's why I wander the clearings, ravines and meadows, to feel something like that. I think each of us has a wild thing in them.

Your wild thing is of the deer family? I ask.

Yes, he says. What about yours?

Hmm, I mutter, mine could be fox-related.

Grandpa looks at me and without a word walks towards the beam supporting the roof. He fetches something out of there.

Here you are, he says.

What's this? I ask.

In reply I hear: I didn't kill it, it was already dead, in a snare.

I unwrap the paper. I see a piece of fox fur. I touch it. I put my fingertip to the little pads of the animal's paw.

I cut off one paw, for good luck, it was many years ago. I detached the rest from the snare and left it in the stream, so the forest could feed on the fox.

It's for good luck, he tells me.

For good luck, I repeat, and place the fox paw in my shirt pocket.

I leave Grandpa in the attic and go off to bed. Ann and Grandma are breathing unevenly.

I fall asleep.

In the morning I'm woken by Ann, who finds the fox paw between us. She doesn't say a word, she just looks now at me, now at the bit of animal.

It's for good luck, I tell her, stroke it.

She strokes it.

JAWS

At the start of the next week we're woken early in the morning by the noises of heavy machinery. A crane is lifting and dropping concrete slabs.

They're concreting the earth, I say.

It'll take revenge, says Grandma.

Like a prosthesis, says Ann.

In the evening the slaughterhouse hill looks like a fortress.

The jaws of the earth have been closed, I jot down in a yellow notebook.

In the morning I can see that where they failed to fit the concrete slabs, concrete mixers are pouring out concrete. That night I dream that it spills onto our field, it's like lava, it goes across the boundary strip, taking our ash trees into its grip.

While the hill is still solidifying, the procedures involving the animals' bodies are set in motion again: the slaughterhouse starts to wheeze, and the animals raise their song.

The smell has its origins in blood and blossoms, I read aloud and delete.

MEDULLA

The earth beneath the hill does not stop working away. A few weeks after the concrete prosthesis was installed one can see that the structure is changing shape, dictated by the soil that's under it.

The hill is opening its jaws again, but now they have concrete teeth as well.

The animals are being unloaded on the main road through the village, so the weight of the vehicles won't burden the ground.

I'm on my way home from the shop. I'm carrying a warm loaf in my hands. I stop to watch for a while. I like to watch, I get it from Grandma.

The cows are large and meaty, I recognize the Simmental breed, Grandpa farmed them for many years. I go closer. Their ample bodies are swaying to the beat of the men's footsteps. I go even closer. I recognize one of the workmen, pushing the cows out of the trailer. It's Staszek.

He notices me and says: This isn't a sight for you.

Oh yes it is, I quip.

I examine the eyes of the cow he's goading. There's no room for calm in them. The cow is trembling. Her body is spattered with shit.

Her body is spattered with shit, I say to Staszek.

Oh yes, he replies.

The cow moves slowly, watchfully, there's something growing inside her, something brewing within her. A few metres on she breaks free of Staszek. The cord slices the skin of his hand. The wound starts bleeding. The animal races ahead.

The concrete in the hill is luring them, it occurs to me.

She runs onto it and disappears.

For seconds or for ages it goes quiet. I'm losing my sense of time. Hush. And after this breach in time everything starts moving, picks up speed and races on.

For fuck's sake, someone shouts, or maybe it's me who shouts it.

In the night one of the slabs has tilted enough to form a deep crevice.

The cow has fallen into the hill.

What the fuck, I hear Staszek say.

I climb up the concrete slabs, stop at a distance of about a dozen metres and watch. With every movement the animal's body fits ever more tightly into the fault. Several men come running from the slaughterhouse. One of them is holding something that looks like a weapon. Shortly after I recognize a bolt gun, probably the same one Staszek showed us, the village kids, many years ago.

Bang.

And silence.

Once again: hush.

The animal's body is divided on the spot. Men go up the hill with pieces of the cow's body, drawing a bloody line on the asphalt. They set the ravenous slaughterhouse dogs, black American pit bulls, loose on what's left in the fault.

The bread has gone cold. I tear off the heel and crush it in my mouth. The sharp crust stabs my palate. I'm eating bread with blood.

Here's the body and the blood, I'm thinking.

I go home.

I tell Ann about what I've seen.

Shhh, not a word to Grandma, please.

I know, she says.

What did they aim at, she asks me that night, in a whisper.

The head, I say, the head, they aim it at the head.

PRAISED

We don't like letting others in to see Grandma, as if the illness were this house's business. Actually, every Sunday Tymoteusz comes by, the parish priest, but he belongs to the ceremony of this loss.

How is Róża? he asks each time.

Flourishing, I reply each time.

He vigilantly goes into Grandma's room.

Jesus Christ be praised, he says.

Grandma mutters something. And she's watching, watching.

I leave them alone.

It doesn't take long.

Abide with God, says the priest at the end.

We shall, I reply.

Once a week the nurse comes from Stary Sad. Her name is Wioletta. She's beautiful. The contours of her body are oval, her lips are full and always coated in red, and her fingernails are a similar red. While her skin is a shade of dark pink. She's entirely bathed in pink.

She has skin like a pig, I whisper to Ann.

Yes, she says, smiles and licks her lips.

I imagine Wioletta standing before a large mirror. She's putting powder on her cheeks and carmine on her lips, she bares her teeth to check it hasn't got onto the white of her incisors.

We need a beauty like her in the face of loss, I'm thinking.

Her hands work gently. No one changes Grandma's drip as tenderly as she does, no one sticks the needle into her sunken veins as she does. She's well acquainted with illness, nothing surprises her, nothing disgusts her, she doesn't say dirty words to death.

I like her, I say each time as she drives off in a yellow Cinquecento.

So do I, I like her too, agrees Ann.

Wioletta is on the side of life, I think.

THE BALTIC

There are other visits too, from those who, at news of the illness, come to look at the dying woman.

They're hungry for the sight, I whisper to Ann.

They're hungry for it, yes, she agrees.

In previous decades they rarely came. On hearing of Grandma's illness, the family renews contact. Although after the death of my parents and aunt it felt as if something had snapped, as though the less immediate family was scared by this sudden tragedy. But not so. Maybe more than twenty years has been enough to forget?

Now they ring up and ask questions. They ring up and invite themselves. I tell them to come, hoping nothing has changed, and no one will show up. I'm wrong. Because the force of attraction of an illness is great and the spectacle of it is curious for the eyes of others.

They keep coming. They bring Ferrero Rochers, chocolate-coated Bird's Milk marshmallows in several flavours, pale oranges, and shining Holy Mothers filled with consecrated water. By now we have lots of shining Marys, and lots of consecrated water too. Just a few more and Grandma's room will start to shine. The visitors also bring towels, for some strange reason they bring my dying grandmother towels.

The Baltic's arrived, the Baltic, I say to Ann, who is staring at the kitchen window. For years I have defined visitors by the name of the region they come from.

And so the Baltic.

Lots of thin people populate the house, and as they kiss us they leave sticky trails of saliva on our faces. They smile. They pat us on the back. They tell us to take them to Grandma.

In the early days I conducted them into the east room.

We're not going to receive visitors in the damp, she decided.

Even at the height of summer the west room stays cool.

We gather at the table, which for this occasion I've made larger, by fetching out the extra leaf that hasn't been used for years.

The visitors talk a lot, they occupy their mouths with words.

It's curious, the people who come to look at the illness cannot talk in language that befits the illness, it occurs to me. They talk about death, intensely, persistently. They weep. Grandma has been through this many times already, she's unmoved.

My grandma is strong, I think.

Tell us something about life, she asks the visitors.

Oh Róża, you've lost weight, someone says.

Oh Róża, what bad luck, someone says.

The will of God, someone says.

Have you any white sugar? someone asks.

The people of the Baltic occupy their mouths with pickles. They have mild, sad faces. I can't blame them for the curiosity that brought the Baltic all the way here.

The illness is strong, the smell of Grandma is sharp, they're suffocating in it.

Shall we go outside? I suggest.

Yes, yes, they say.

They've had to learn the rules of this house at lightning speed: agree to everything, give way to the illness, don't raise your voice.

We go out of the front door.

They light Marlboros.

They weep.

Danube licks the hands of the Baltic.

The Baltic weeps over Grandma's fate. I'd like to tell the people from the Baltic coast that it pisses me off when they come and weep. Meanwhile they watch, on the alert. They're scared. This fear has a smell. Their acrid sweat cuts the air. I want to tell them to disappear. But I hear the words flowing from my lips: We have plum cake, maybe you'll come inside again?

They come in, because they're hungry.

Ann serves them a cake baked last night. It's moist, with crumble topping. Sweetness spreads on our palates.

Grandpa starts to talk about replacing the roof.

The Baltic listens.

The people of the Baltic stir their cups of coffee in synchrony, flicking dark droplets from their spoons as they strike the edge of the china.

It forms a glassy tune.

I'm watching Grandma, who's holding a mug of milky tea. I don't yet know that in a week she won't be able to do that.

She winks at me.

Grandma is beautiful when in fatal illness she winks at me.

LUCK

Following the afternoon meal, Grandma decides to get up.

I'm getting up, she says.

I doubt it, I think.

I go over to help her, sure it won't work. But she does get up. She stands steadily on her feet. She tells me to pass her some warm clothing. I hand her a pair of tights, trousers and a polo neck made of alpaca wool, which Ann brought for her. I massage greasy cream into Grandma's face. I undo her plait, her hair smells of the birch water that I rubbed into the luminous skin on her head last night. I plait it again.

Maybe she's getting ready for church, I think.

I'm ready, she says.

Where are we going? I ask.

Into the forest.

So I go with her, very slowly, into the summer forest.

Grandma is alive to the beauty of the birch bark, the dampness of the moss and the wind jostling the aspen leaves. She does it in defiance of the illness working away inside her.

She belongs to the forest, to this earth, I'm thinking.

On a broad meadow at the very top of the village it occurs to me that anyone who has never been in a forest with a dying person is lucky, but also that anyone who has never been in a forest with a dying person is unlucky too.

OPIOID

Grandma brings a beautiful word home from Stary Sad. She repeats it several times. The word works in her mouth, it's rounded, but there are points of tension in it that soften at the relevant spots.

Shortly after we're convinced the word not only resonates, but does something else too – it lets light into the veins. Lots of light.

ALLUVIAL SOIL

Profusion. It's hard to find another word to describe what's happening to the body of the village. The second half of July was damp and August is starting the same way.

The plants have no time to shake off the dew. The mown grass on the hilltop is rotting. From the forest a wide tongue of mist emerges in tandem with the dawn and licks the village.

The greenery is heavily laden.

The burdock leaves are immense. I think about their white roots working away in the alluvial soil. I imagine them spreading in earth the colour of anthracite and uniting with the roots of other plants. I imagine the white roots growing, winding up the village, and if they were pulled out, the bright spine of the valley would be exposed.

The rain slows down the movements of insects. The sun only appears for a moment to cast a touch of warmth onto our bodies and the body of May. It lasts too briefly to allow the bees to leave their hives.

They're eating up the honey they brought in themselves, says Grandpa.

What about the mother bee? I ask.

She's anxious, it must be cramped and stuffy for her, he says, drawing the head of a match along the striking strip, then raises it and sets it to the tip of his cigarette. The flame touches the Klub he's holding in his mouth.

The mother bee, there's revolution gearing up inside her, which will devour her, I write in my notebook.

The movements of the large animals are slow. The dampness sends them to sleep. Our cows are lying by the boundary strip, warmth is escaping from their bodies, they're steaming.

It's different for plants, they gain from the damp.

The songbirds are busy not emitting sounds. On the other side of the village white storks fly down to the parish chairwoman's meadows, where they dance around the crickets and frogs.

The boys from the edge of the forest, known to the village as the Swarts, have carried a white goose onto the roof of the barn.

It's standing there shining.

It's shining.

We're walking about as if in a fever.

Grandma's room is dark in spite of the white walls. The boughs of the pear tree have come up to the window, the leaves are large, malachite. The fruits are weighed down by rain.

Steamy.

The damp must be good for Grandma, look, I say to Ann.

Grandma raises a hand, my grandma, whom something is eating away from inside, who has been in a state of emergency for months, raises her hand, though she hasn't raised her hand for many days now.

ONE TO ONE

Look, the earth is hungry over there too, says Grandpa, it's been moving.

He's on the veranda, leaning against the balustrade. He's smoking a Klub. And gazing ahead.

Moving? Where? I ask.

Over there, he says, pointing at the hill opposite.

The sound of church bells rings out.

It has started, look, he says.

Just above the parish chairwoman's boundary strip the earth is splitting. From our veranda it looks as if the bluff has parted its lips, it looks like a wrinkling human face.

This village, I think to myself, must have been founded on a large slippery boulder.

I'm off, says Grandpa.

He goes to fire up the tractor and hitches a cart to it. Soon I see him speeding along a narrow thread of asphalt, until he disappears in the brushwood that grows along the banks of the stream. He emerges on the other side of May. He drives up to one of the houses. Children come spilling out of it. On their little backs they have backpacks. The colourful dots mix together. Grandpa seats them in the cart. Soon he disappears again in the brushwood growing along the stream. The machine falls silent at the school, which is on our side, the safe side. There, so I guess, they've made a temporary shelter.

And the movement begins.

Tractors are moving, and cars, and animals are being led out of the stables. The poultry is being set free – who has time to think of the poultry when the earth is dancing?

Evacuation? asks Ann, who has just got up. She's still full of sleep.

Evacuation, look.

The lips of the earth are moist, I think to myself.

I'm off, I say to Ann.

Soon after, on my way by now, I imagine how Ann can see the comma of my body as it disappears in the thicket by the stream, and then stops outside Rybowicz's door.

I knock.

He doesn't answer.

I enter. I wade through empty beer cans.

I find him sleeping.

The earth has been moving, I say, standing in the doorway of the cramped kitchen.

He opens his eyes and for a second longer I can see the other side of life, the sleep in them. He quickly shakes it off, like an animal beset by horseflies.

Already? he asks, as if he's been expecting it.

Yes, I reply.

We go out into the yard. We examine the bluff above his cottage. From our veranda we can see how the lips of the earth are widening in a smile, and very soon, in a day or two, the bluff will collapse.

I'm waiting for you, you cold bitch, he says to the earth. Come on then, he says, one to one.

He turns towards me and says something that doesn't surprise me: I'm staying put.

I didn't come here to object, I think.

Yes, I say.

What about the animals? I ask.

Take them, he says.

I let the Keeshond off its chain. He calls it Hound. I've never seen it running free. It sets off into the village. Its body movements bear witness to the fact that it has lived on a chain – it wants everything now and all at once.

I enter the stable, where there's a Polish Red cow. I undo the chain. I lead her into the daylight.

Look after yourself, I say to Rybowicz over my shoulder.

The devil takes care of his own, he replies.

I walk down the valley with the cow, to the line of the stream. She plunges her muzzle in the wet. She laps as if her belly were bottomless. She raises her muzzle and waits for me to move. She lets herself be led as if she's always been led by me. Outside the house I tie her to an old plum tree in the orchard.

I fetch a curry comb from the stable and I clean her. Dried shit falls to the grass. With each successive stroke here and there hair falls off too, her smooth, chafed skin is visible. I go up to her muzzle and look into it. I put my muzzle to the cow's muzzle. We mingle breaths.

Children emerge from the stream, it's the ones who live at the very top of the hill that's sinking.

Good morning, Miss! they shout to me.

Good morning! I shout back.

Each of them is holding a small animal under an arm. They're carrying: a cat, a hen, a hamster. They're walking towards the school. Their conversation goes quiet around the bend. Then a white goose emerges from the stream. It waddles onto the asphalt and stops. It looks around, as if considering which way the children have gone. It's drawn down to the village. It waddles off in that direction, rhythmically shifting the weight of its body from one foot to the other. It's running after the flock.

BIRDS

In her illness Grandma has whims.

More of the world, she says.

So I read her poems, and lately books about birds too. She likes both of them. She's hungry for them. She demands poetry. She demands information about birds, she asks: Make the call of the bird you're reading about.

There's not much difference between poetry and descriptions of birds, she says one night.

Yes, I admit.

Grandma knows a lot about poetry, she's shown an interest, she has wanted to know what do I do, what am I dealing with. A few years ago she asked: Is it possible to live off that?

I lied and said that it is. Grandma knows little about my work for people across the ocean. I've learnt not to write code in her presence, because she thinks I'm writing poems, and she wants me to read them to her. Hence the makeshift office I prepared after moving here, in my old room in the attic, right next to Grandpa's collection of antlers.

In the face of the illness Grandma wants to know more about the world. Today she has chosen words about birds.

Read, she asks.

'The jay,' I start solemnly.

I read: 'Vigilant and shy, difficult to approach. Omnivore; summer diet includes a good many eggs and young of small birds. Nests usually in tree.'

And what is its call? asks Grandma.

I look in the guide for information. I run my gaze over the description and reply: It's complicated.

What is it? she asks again.

I summarize: If it's a warning, it's 'kschaah!', but that can also be an advertising call. Sometimes it gives a descending mew, very like a buzzard's, and that sounds like 'piyeh'. But listen to this, it's interesting, I say, sometimes it mimics the cackle of its arch-enemy, the goshawk, and cries 'kya-kya-kya...'

Kya-kya-kya-kya-kya, emerges from Grandma's lips.

She opens her mouth a little, I can see her tongue working away, as she gently presses it to her lower teeth.

Kya-kya-kya fills the room.

DEVIL

The devil has taken care of his own, I write in my notebook.

The bluff collapsed in the night. From the veranda it looks as if the lower lip of the earth has lost its muscles, gone floppy and wilted.

Rybowicz's cottage is underground. Men from the valley have been there since early morning, and the emergency services have come from Stary Sad.

An anthill, I say to Ann and point at the peculiar mound on which the people are working.

Grandma taps on the window of the room, the one by the veranda. I know she's curious. I escort her from the room into the fresh air and seat her in an armchair lined with pillows.

Eyes, says Grandma.

I hand her the binoculars.

She watches.

How sad, she says, saddest of all for the animal, that dog of his, Hound, he's sitting on the roof now, like the white goose does at the Swart house. Such a misfortune. The roof's up above the ground, and the dog's growling at the men digging out the house. What a sight! And how sad for his soul – no one will bury Rybowicz at the cemetery. Not in the church way, not the religious way. He hasn't been to confession, he turned his back on the Church years ago, he boasted of it. He carved a message on his front door at the time: I believe in pleasure and alcohol.

I can remember that hazy inscription.

Late that afternoon they extract Rybowicz's body.

It's taken up by the machinery of the funeral parlour from the city. And he's never heard of again.

KIWANO

Ann and I are doing a lot for this loss, it occurs to me. Sometimes we experiment, we bring home exotic fruits from town, kinds we've never eaten before: granadilla, kiwano, tamarillo. Grandma is interested in the colours and textures. Sometimes she has us read to her about the countries they're from. And asks what sort of birds they have in those countries. She gets us to imitate the calls of those birds. But she doesn't put the fruit in her mouth.

No, she says.

But there is a food she won't refuse: pigeon broth. And Grandpa – who avoids Grandma's illness, to whom any ceremony around illness is alien, the man who refuses to know anything about illness, or touch anything that's ill – kills a bird at Grandma's command, he dresses it and sets about making broth. He singes the bird's body over burning meths to remove the last of the feathers. Then he cuts it into smaller pieces. Crumbles it. Pigeon flesh has a subtle flavour. He puts the meat in a pot with onion seared on the range and makes stock, adding celery, parsley, carrot, allspice, bay leaves and garlic. He crushes the garlic in his hands. He smells of it for many days after.

Eat, cries Grandma as soon as she smells the aroma.

Grandma laps up the broth, she smacks her lips as she eats the bird. Her hands regain flexibility, her mouth opens and closes. A chunk of meat raises her Adam's apple.

It's good, says Grandma and lowers her head to lick the plate clean.

Nothing can be wasted, she says, and smacks her lips again and again.

In late August we start to run out of pigeons.

Grandpa won't take money from the villagers for honey any more. He swaps honey for birds, fledglings best of all. For a one-litre jar of honeydew honey it's three pigeons; for a jar of May honey it's two birds; for a small bottle of propolis in alcohol it's one bird.

Grandma's illness is hungry, soon it'll have devoured all the pigeons in the valley.

Grandma loves birds and poems, I note down.

TAMARISK

Grandma jabs the index finger of her right hand into the *Collins Bird Guide*. It opens at pages two hundred and ninety and two hundred and ninety-one. I shove the book under her nose. I point a fingernail at one of the birds.

'Red-rumped wheatear,' I read.

Red-rumped wheatear, repeats Grandma.

Read it, she urges me.

I summarize: Length fourteen and a half to sixteen centimetres. Breeds mostly at lower levels on flat, sandy or clayey heaths or in more barren, stony semi-desert, at times among tamarisk bushes and scanty low vegetation. Spends much time on ground. Resident. Food insects. Nests in ground hole.

Tamarisk, whispers Grandma.

Tamarisk, yes, I confirm.

And its voice? she asks.

I find the information in the text and try to repeat it.

'Prrit,' I blurt, making my mouth do gymnastics: 'Prrit.'

'Prrit,' repeats Grandma, 'prrit.'

LIGHT

Where did you get it? I ask Ann, touching the scar on her right cheek that's only visible in the light.

For ages she doesn't respond, then she touches the scar, takes my hand and puts it to the skin of her cheek, as if by this gesture to convince me that the scar exists.

Finally she answers: I wanted to have a memento of the light that surprised me one morning over there, far away – she nods to the east. Nothing ever reflected the light like a fragment of that mirror. I touched my cheek with it. Sometimes I forget how much strength I have in my hands. Sometimes I don't notice that I'm raising a hand to myself. I forget myself in it. Just like Róża when she scratches herself. I didn't think the mirror was sharp enough to pierce the skin so I'd have to have stitches.

We're alike in this, in raising a hand to ourselves, I'm thinking.

I did it for the light. But I'll let you in on a secret, it's not about the light, it's about the shade that follows it. For me it's always about the shade, she adds.

A mark left by light, I think.
You're beautiful with it, I tell Ann that night.

SWARM

Hot weather.

The bees are restless, says Grandpa.

There's trouble brewing, I'm thinking.

I find Grandma by the window of the west room, the one that looks onto the slaughterhouse.

She's gazing at the pall-like mass that is gradually changing formation, shimmering with black and gold. The swarm is working away in the upper corner of the window as if in a trance.

The living has come to Grandma's kingdom of its own accord.

There, she says, and points at the mother bee.

She's emaciated. Is that to be capable of flight? Or to be capable of leading the swarm out of Grandpa's hive? What were they short of there? Food? Air? Space?

The transom window is ajar, it's through there that scouts have entered and inspected the structure of the room, to return to the swarm and give their report: suitable for a new home or not suitable. Others have flown further off to check out narrow holes in trees, crevices in the trunks of hornbeams and beeches, chinks beneath the thresholds of old houses, or abandoned hives where mice have found shelter by now.

I call Ann, who puts down an album about Asian temples. She comes over.

Look, I say.

She looks.

She freezes. I want to go on watching the kingdom that has come to call on us, but I know that at any moment the mother bee might give the order for take-off.

Loss is close by, I'm thinking.

Grandpa comes up to the swarm from the direction of the orchard. He hasn't thrown on a shirt.

I open the window and ask him: Aren't you afraid?

We're of the same smell, he replies.

His suntanned body has already accepted venom. Now he feels no fear, he has gathered a swarm dozens of times, he knows how calm a swarm is when it's in search of a new home. He's holding a bucket of well water. He uses some stems of tansy picked near the house to make an aspergillum and sprinkles the bees with it. They become quieter. He gathers them with the herb stalks. He plunges his hands into the bees that have stayed on the frame and transfers them to a basket that we use in autumn to pick bunches of purple grapes.

The bees move as if hypnotized, taking their place by the mother. Once the swarm is in shape again, Grandpa takes it down to the cellar, where the smells of maturing wine, last year's fruits and vegetables mingle: grey reinette apples, potatoes, swedes. The swarm finds its way into a darkened corner.

The cool air will send them to sleep, says Grandpa.

He comes out to prepare the hive.

A few hours later I come back and help him to transfer the body of the swarm. I put the mother bee into the hive, cleansed of cobwebs and dust, which Grandpa burnt out with living fire, as he calls it, and rubbed with salvia. The worker bees can tell where she is, and start their procession. Their march is like a mathematical equation. Everything adds up, everything cooperates. They reach the hive and start to establish their own order in there.

I put my head to it, I cock an ear, I want to hear the return to life, the hum.

At this point Grandpa speaks.

You know, he begins, and pauses.

I look at him, I don't interrupt him because I know his ways, his respect for the word, his silence. He's not in the habit of talking without need, unless it's going to be a tale about deer antlers, about the forest, but here, I sense, it's about something else. His speech, if it comes into being, always serves a purpose.

He says: It never occurred to me to give her anything here. For it to say in the documents that this is hers too – the house, the woods, the fields, the apiary. She never asked, she never wanted anything. I could have done it. With her illness, I'm thinking about how she has lived, and I can see that I took her like an object. She came from a place that no longer existed. Her family home was underwater, just like the rest of her village, which was flooded. Once, before the betrothal, she took me to the reservoir and pointed at its eastern half. She told me to close my eyes. I did. And she began to describe the whole village, house by house, the shop, the church, the groves, the places where the most beautiful saffron milk caps grew. Everything the water had covered. She spoke so that under my eyelids I could see it all. And finally she said she had nothing to go back to, that where she now lived she wasn't at home, that she wanted to build something to call home. She asked me to take her. I took her, because that's what she wanted and she was beautiful. But now I can see that she clung to me because she had nothing, and she's passing on with nothing. And she has had to bury her own children too. Sometimes I think it's only you that keeps her alive, and so do the birds, so they do.

POEM

That afternoon I tell Grandma what I saw in the apiary. She asks me questions. She's interested in the colours, the details. She listens. Suddenly she raises a hand. She looks at it.

My body's going off, she says.

And slowly lowers the hand to the eiderdown. She falls asleep.

She wakes before night. Ann escorts her to the heated bathroom. I stay in the room and change the sheets. Under her pillow I find a piece of paper folded in four. I see the stamp of the oncology hospital. It's her diagnosis. It occurs to me that it's the diagnosis for all of us, for the whole house, for each body and each thing that's here.

I put it back in place. I straighten the pillow.

Ann brings Grandma back from the bathroom. Grandma smells nice. Ann is good to her, she's kind, she carries out her wishes. A frequent wish of Grandma's nowadays is for us to scratch her – raking, as she calls it.

I scratched, Ann whispers in my ear at night, I've got her flesh under my fingernails.

She holds out her long-fingered hands towards the moonlight.

ASH TREES

We're hiding behind the thick trunks of the ash trees that grow on the boundary strip, spying on the men. They're scorched by the sun, they have an August layer of heat on them.

Their bodies must be warm, says Ann.

Yes, I reply.

The muscles on their bared torsos are gleaming.

The slaughterhouse is sliding down the slope.

The earth is just, I'm thinking.

The animals are being taken for slaughter. They're not in a hurry, they're indolent, they must be unaware that their bodies will be mixed up, their meat will become a common body that the men will carry off far from here, perhaps as soon as tomorrow in the cold dawn.

I describe to Grandma the colours of the cows led into the slaughterhouse today: white-and-cream, copper, black.

Colours are still on the side of life, it occurs to me.

And the workmen? she asks.

They were wearing brown, I say.

WONDERS

That night I read to my women about the lyrebird.

It can copy the sound of a table saw or a power saw, I say.

Grandma arranges her lips to imitate that sound, but doesn't make the noise of any machine.

She says: What wonders, wonders.

FOREST

Grandma sleeps, lulled by morphine. On the floor of her room I have spread out the books that for years on end were the only ones in this house. Many are about cattle breeding and beekeeping. I turn the yellowed pages, here and there I see words added in pencil, and also sketches of animals drawn by Grandpa's hand. Pictures have always spoken to him more forcefully than words.

The door to the hall is wide open, the door to Grandma's room is slightly ajar.

This place needs air, some wind, I'm thinking.

I hear something shuffling across the floor, and a scream like a child's at the door of the room. I open it fully. Azrael has come here from May, from the village battleground, covered in blood. His left ear is bitten, his left eye is coated in gore. He's trailing a back paw behind him.

I look.

I reach my hands towards him.

He hisses and runs forwards.

He leaves a rusty trail behind him. He crosses the spread-out books and goes towards the bed and sleeping Grandma. He tries to scramble onto it. He does it in silence. After a few unsuccessful attempts he sits still. He's looking at me.

I'm afraid of his blood, I want to protect Grandma's body from it.

Help him, she says as if through her sleep.

I fold a checked blanket and place it under his paws. He starts moving. Up this step he manages to get onto the bed. The eiderdown sags beneath his weight. The animal locates Grandma's belly and lies down on it. The white bedding assumes some red. Grandma reaches out a hand to the cat's head, he rubs against it, she touches something wet, raises her fingers to her eyes and inspects them. She puts the blood to her nose and sniffs.

Forest and wind, she says.

Yes, I reply.

Grandma puts her hand back on the cat's head. She stays in this position.

Shhh, she says to the cat and falls asleep.

The animal falls asleep too.

A chapter of the book about cattle reproduction and how to inseminate cows by Władysław Głód has taken on colour.

MEAT

Staszek knocks at the front door. I open it. He's brought something. In one hand he has a shopping bag from the Lewiatan supermarket, in the other the head of a calf wrapped in plastic – an Uckermärker. I'd recognize the set of the eyes and ears and that broad muzzle anywhere.

Livers for Róża, he says, and hands me the bag.

He has brought Grandma a piece of a large animal that he must recently have cut out with his own hands.

The meat stinks.

The meat of a large animal won't go down Grandma's throat, I think.

Thank you, I say.

Before Sunday I'll bring a bit of pig, he says.

Thank you, I say.

He turns away. He goes down to the main road. On the asphalt Danube catches up with him, he's scented blood. Staszek fetches out a penknife, cuts an ear off the calf's head and tosses it into the orchard for him. Danube chews the calf's ear under the dry boughs of a plum tree.

I watch the dog, following his movements. The chase has sculptured his muscles. His fangs are snow-white, as if hewn from moonstones. I call him. He runs up. There's blood and hair on his nose. I'm off my guard and his great big tongue lashes my face.

DEEP INSIDE

For the past few weeks Grandma's hands have been occupied, they're touching a living thing that was close to death. Where he was bitten, the cat has lost his fur. Now you can stroke the pale skin there. Grandma likes that. The cat is patient and indulgent with her hands, he allows the sweeping strokes that, I think, bring him some relief.

Over the weeks since being bitten Azrael has been slower, he's more attentive, looking deep inside. He can't hear. He hardly ever leaves Grandma. During the day he only goes outside briefly, where under the vine he offers the earth the leftovers from his body. He returns at a run, as if unsure Grandma will take him back again. She does, and he finds the spot under the thick eiderdown where her belly is located, lies down there and goes to sleep. Now and then he wakes, starts up the engine of his larynx, purrs and kneads Grandma's belly through the eiderdown.

Grandma's hands are getting thinner and thinner, but more and more occupied, I think to myself, that's a good thing.

SHEEN

Grandpa avoids Grandma's illness, ceremony around illness is alien to him, he refuses to know anything about illness, or to touch anything that's ill. But he wants to have Grandma within earshot.

Grandma's place is at home. Things have to be done to make sure Grandma has warmth. She deserves warmth, he says.

The men from Stary Sad carry the great radiator ribs made in Italy into the hall. They're strong and agile. They don't need help, but Grandpa assists them, he wants to do it. Qualified professionals will have to be brought in from outside the village. There's no one left here who specializes in what we need.

It's August, the winter is still far off, we've time to install them. There's still time to do it just so, says Grandpa.

How so? I ask.

With a sheen, he says.

It's to look smart, he says.

The wind and the damp are to have no way in, he says.

It's to be warm, he continues, when Grandma sets her bare foot on the kitchen floor, the floor is to warm it. And after a while all the floors will be like radiators, so you'll want to walk about the house just for the sake of walking. You'll want to stroll around for the sake of strolling around. Grandma won't be sorry she can't go outside, it'll be so good for her in here, so nice.

SWART

From the veranda we can see the hillside opposite. The hot weather has halted the movements of the earth there. Or maybe something that was meant to occur has simply occurred – the devil has taken care of his own.

There's a swarm of children under the parish chairwoman's cherry tree. They're climbing onto the branches and filling their bulging bellies with sweetness.

I haven't touched that tree for almost thirty years, I say to Ann.

Why not? she asks.

One summer Grandpa took me over there, I say. He perched me on the spreading cherry tree. I ate some fruit. I spat out the stones. A boy from the edge of the forest sat down beside me, the older brother of the ones the locals call the Swarts. They called him that too, it started with him. His eyes are like coal. He stared at me the way a dog stares. He moved close to me. Those boys, the Swarts, can be spotted by the fact that they don't blink, and he didn't blink then. The rough bark was scratching my skin. I was wearing shorts and sandals. Grandpa hadn't put a vest on me. In those days I didn't think of the body as something that entices. It just was, and that's all. I was about six. And when he was close, when I could smell an earthy odour from his mouth, he asked: What have you got there? He pointed at my chest, which I had smeared with fruit juice. Juice, I replied. Then he said: Give it here. He leant forwards and put his mouth to my nipple. He moved his tongue against it several times. I started to rumble inside. I told him in a whisper to leave off. It went on for hours and hours, or maybe a few seconds. Grandpa was talking to the parish chairwoman on the boundary strip, his hands were occupied with banknotes for propolis. He didn't see a thing. The boy pinched my nipple with his teeth. He bit it. After a million years he moved away from me. He licked his lips. He coughed something up. He didn't spit it out. He swallowed it. He smiled and said: There's a lot to lick up in you.

What a prick, says Ann, what a prick, and lays a cool hand on my neck.

SKIN

Here. This is where you're going wrong, says Ann.

She's pointing at my windpipe. Ann knows what she's saying, hers went wrong many years ago. She knows the symptoms. At first I think she's trying to give my body an excuse, trying to protect me in the face of Grandma's illness.

For several months I've been gaining weight.

I'm swelling.

My thighs, buttocks and belly are growing.

I'm growing on my back and breasts.

My fingers are growing. They look as if hornets had stung them.

I'm getting heavier and I'm carrying this weight of mine around the house. I'm starting to accept it. I like it.

There's a consolation in the fact that while Grandma is dwindling something else here, in this house, is gaining flesh. But with it comes drowsiness, though a sense of duty tears me from its grip. The day's rituals have their set times: washing, eating, dispensing medicine, washing, eating, dispensing medicine, washing, eating, dispensing medicine, smoking cigarettes, writing code. And also reading to myself and reading to Grandma. And sleeping.

Here. This is where you're going wrong, says Ann.

I gather my strength and early one sultry morning I go to the clinic in Stary Sad. My blood is taken by a young man, he says he's a trainee. My veins won't cooperate with his stabbing. He shakes his head above me.

He calls the nurse and says: It's all hidden inside her, it's impossible to get a needle into her.

The nurse taps my vein, which slowly swells, and meanwhile she tells me to clench my fist. She inserts the needle. I watch the blood as it fills the test tube, it's as dark as Grandpa's wine, it occurs to me.

A few days after the blood sample is taken, I'm certain.

Here, this is where I'm going wrong, I say, showing Grandma my neck area.

From now on, before feeding Grandma, before sticking the morphine patch on her body, we, Ann and I, place little white pills on each other's tongues. Ann puts a dose of two hundred micrograms on my tongue, and I put a dose of twenty micrograms on her tongue.

SCENT HOUND

The hall belongs to Danube. His claws strike the floorboards. The little hall divides the house. To the east it's warm, to the west it's cool.

The night promises to be restless. We can see this in the animal's activity, in his whimpering, in his abrupt charges towards the glazed veranda door.

His heightened activity fills the interior of the house. I'm afraid for his body, which reacts with convulsions to the thunder heralding a storm.

The scent hound who's afraid of thunder, says Grandpa, shaking his head over him.

Open the door to this room, let him come in, says Grandma.

Danube comes in and rests his head on the bed.

He's looking at Grandma.

We let him look. His eye movements are alert. He's whimpering.

There's impatience in him, I say to Ann.

Fear, she adds.

Shade, I say.

Panic, says Ann.

Something wild, I say.

And something human, says Ann.

Look, he's got white hair on his muzzle, I say.

Look there, says Ann, pointing at his belly, he's grown a lump. I touch the growth. It's soft, full of something fluid. Danube turns his head towards me and bares his teeth, he makes this gesture theatrically, but without sound, as if the wild thing in him were prompting him to defend himself, but the domesticated thing had taken his voice away.

He stays like that for ages with his lips raised. His expression is menacing, warning. Gradually he calms down. First his lower lip goes back in place, followed a little later by the right half of the upper one. Although there's already forgiveness for that touch in his eyes, the left half refuses to drop, as if it were stuck to his gums. Ann touches it with a finger, a gesture that causes the lip to drop at last.

Danube jumps onto Grandma's bed. By turns he licks her hand and reaches with his tongue for the lump on his own belly.

The storm is moving beyond the ridge, disappearing to the north and raining into the reservoir. Danube is beside Grandma, shaking and quivering.

The nearby forest falls silent.

The night takes possession of us.

In the morning I find the dog lying next to Grandma, occasionally he jolts his paws, as if running after prey. His jaw is moving, maybe he's grabbing hold of something.

He's having skittish dreams, I note down.

I kiss him on the muzzle, which he snaps at his dream. In it he's bringing us animal heads from the slaughterhouse. As last spring, at Whitsuntide, when the lawn was strewn with cow heads.

The scent hound who brings in carrion, said Grandpa, shaking his head over him.

That morning I picked up the cow heads and laid them out on the boundary strip separating us from the slaughterhouse. With time the number of heads has increased, and there are pig and horse heads there now too. Nature works on them in its own special way. It does a bit of decomposing, some gnawing, and polishes them clean.

The animal heads will soon reach the first boughs of the ash trees, I'm thinking.

The dung flies feed on them, and shine in the sunlight. The smell from them ripens and releases the aroma of decay.

Danube wakes up and changes position, lying on his back. The dog's body is the size of Grandma, shrunken by illness. She goes on sleeping. I lay my hands on their two bodies. Both here and here the ribcage rises and falls, rises and falls, rises and falls.

DEWLAP

What do you want that animal dreck for, what do you want those heads for? asks Staszek, who has brought some meat. All that has to be hidden, out of people's sight. But your mutt drags it around the village. Fucking hell, people have seen it, he says. Those are the slaughterhouse's heads, eh.

They're our heads now, I reply.

He goes on, as if he hasn't heard me: One night I'll bring some petrol and set fire to all that animal dreck on the boundary. It'll go up in smoke. Fucking hell, it'll turn to ashes.

Those heads belong to us now, I repeat, and add: They've been yours already.

Silence.

He drops his gaze. He raises his bag to my eyes.

Tenderloin, he says.

The meat he brings stinks, the meat he cuts out of the bodies of large animals and offers as a sacrifice to Grandma will not go down her throat. She always insists I give it to Danube.

Thank you, I say.

Tomorrow I'll bring the dewlap, he says.

Possibly, I say, you've paid off your debt by now.

That debt has no end, he says.

All right, I reply.

I don't want to deprive him of his penance.

Tomorrow the dewlap, he says, and turns towards the road.

His hands are bathed in blood. He puts them under Danube's muzzle.

Lick, he tells him.

Danube doesn't refuse blood.

He licks.

MEETING

Staszek and Grandpa are unable to meet. They're like two magnets that repel each other, but I prefer to think about it as if each is a separate planet, and they cannot meet because that would mean disaster.

I'm not worried that one will attack the other, I've grown used to the idea of some impossible configurations in the valley, and this is one of them. They do not seem to exist for each other. Once only Grandpa raised his head when I mentioned Staszek, his penance, and his meat.

The son of a whore and Satan, he said.

And so he hung this curse over Staszek. Maybe it's about the blood from the slaughterhouse? Or the noises that come from it. And it could be about the smell, which as we all know in this house, in this neighbourhood, is a constant reminder of death; I imagine it would be a fine thing, wonderful to live for just a while without that smell, so pungent that every day Grandpa goes up onto the ridge, and there, in the topmost field, he turns to face the reservoir, for a brief moment to breathe a little air that doesn't mean anything, but just is.

HOUND

All trace of Rybowicz has gone, but not the memory. The reminder of him is Hound, who roams the village. He has become the dog of everyone in the valley. Every day he dines at a different house. It's always roughly the same – he appears first thing at the garden gate, keeping a safe distance and staring at the front door. The householders bring out their leftovers for him, sometimes he gets a better morsel from a pig-sticking, or else he gets the scraps from birds slain for Sunday lunch: the red combs of roosters, turkey heads or duck feet.

Hound won't let anyone near him. He accepts food, but gives nothing in return, keeps no company, doesn't bark, doesn't attach himself to anyone. He avoids the slaughterhouse. Possibly, I think, he's afraid of the pit bulls or the people.

No one knows where he spends the night, I say to Ann, who has brought out a bowl of water for him and some pig bones from which, specially with Hound in mind, Grandpa hasn't sucked the marrow.

Imagine, she says, that he is the night, so he's everywhere.

Yes, I say, I like that idea.

BLOSSOMING

Look, says Grandpa.

He puts something that looks like an American blueberry on the *Stary Sad Echo* that's lying open on the table. I go closer. I look. I recognize the blood-filled abdomen of a tick.

Where's the head? I ask.

Still in there, says Grandpa.

He rolls up his trouser leg and exposes a white calf. It occurs to me that the men here, in the valley, never wear shorts, so from the waist up their bodies are tanned, and from the waist down they're as white as corpses.

We have to get it out, I say.

Here you are, says Grandpa, handing me a penknife.

I dig around in my Grandpa's body, which smells of many years of life, of dampness and animals.

The blade wounds his flesh but fails to reach the arachnid's head. I fetch a pair of tweezers. I gouge it out along with a small piece of my grandpa's flesh. I douse the wound in medical spirit.

There'll be a scar. He has lots of those, and so do I, I'm thinking.

Look, says Grandpa the day after.

There's a red patch spreading on his calf.

It's blossoming inside you, I say, we must stop it.

It'll melt away, he says.

He digs in his trouser pocket and pulls out a crumpled packet of Klubs. He offers me one and says: Not a word to Grandma.

MOUTH

Ann's upper lip is swelling. August won't ease up. I rather think the hot temperature annoys the insects. This week in the apiary three swarms followed the mothers out.

Our bodies exude heat.

I'm holding a mirror before Ann's face, I'm watching as she carefully smears soft soap on her lip, swollen by a bee sting.

Does it hurt? I ask.

Yes, she replies.

On the veranda I unfold the sofa bed that's been moved there for the duration of the summer heatwave and spread out a sheet. I help Grandma to sit down. Ann comes and sits down too. The shadow of a pear tree separates us from the strong sunbeams. The sunshine is growing. In a few hours it'll reach the surface of the material and our bodies. I hand Grandma the pear tree's soft fruit, she takes it in her bony hands, asks for a spoon and scrapes out the pulp. The sweet smell entices the wasps.

I touch Ann's brow, it's burning hot, and her face is flushed from the sting.

Nothing more will happen in the village today, I think, as I look at the hillsides put to sleep by the heat. Grandpa has gone to the other side of the village, to the meadows, where I turned out the cows this morning. He can be spotted from the veranda, his movements are slow and searching. Now and then he kneels on the ground and tears something from it. I know what, because this morning he betrayed to me that he knows how to cure Grandma. The parish chairwoman was told by her daughter-in-law, and the daughter-in-law read online, that dandelion root helps with cancer.

I tell my women about it.

Yes, they say.

I bring Grandma a thin shirt, I help her to remove her top made of artificial material. Exposed, her body won't let us forget about the illness that's working away to its own rhythm. We lie down side by side.

We're lulled to sleep by the close air and the rustling of leaves.

I dream of a great fire on the boundary strip. I dream that the animal heads are burning: cow, pig and horse heads. I dream that the fire is nipping at the live, moist bodies of the ash trees, finally it takes them over and rambles through them. The tongues of fire are hungry, that's what I'm thinking in this dream. The tongues of fire are licking the beams of our barns, catching hay and straw in their fire, taking over the rack wagon and the tractor. They take over the vine, and there the tongues of flame are now close to the forest. I dream that the fire is licking the border of the forest. From there it's close to everything.

I can feel a tongue of flame in my throat.

I wake up.

The sun has had time to change position.

I raise my head, the feverish heat has taken me over too. I look at the bodies of my women. The sun has had no mercy, it has entered their skin wherever it could. I inspect my right hand, after gently removing Ann's hand from it. Where it lay I see white skin, she took the sting of the sun for me. I look at her face, covered in redness. The soap on her upper lip has dried out by now and is crumbling onto her vest.

I shift my gaze to Grandma's heated body; the way she has arranged it, the sun has only managed to work on her left arm. It has touched her with pink and brought out freckles.

I get up, and fetch a jar of sour cherry compote from the kitchen, abandoned by the light. On the way I grab hold of some skin cream.

I stop in the veranda doorway and I start to hoot: Whoooo hooo, whoooo hooo.

I wake them up with it.

I observe the way they touch their own bodies, they have to get used to the patches of red and pink that at night, so I suspect, will start to emit warmth combined with pain. But not yet.

Now, above the western forest, the day is ending. The sunset is blood-red, a portent of rain.

I can feel the compote in my gullet, then further down, as if it were travelling along my veins into every corner of my body.

I smear Sudocrem on Grandma's arm. She submits to it. As I finish, I touch Ann's lips. She smears cream on my dry face. I can't open my eyelids, it weighs them down.

For months I've associated the smell of the cream with Grandma's body, with her soft, slippery crannies. And now we're sitting here on an August evening coated in it, so we're also covered in the smell of illness, and from today it'll be the smell of solace too.

The cows' hooves resound on the stone slabs below the veranda, they're returning to the stable, driven by Grandpa. Earlier they crossed the stream, which August has depleted, plunged their muzzles in it and drew coolness and moisture into their bodies.

I look at Grandma. She's taking deep breaths, as if to store them, as if she can sense a change of weather. Her hand is so thin that she can reach the whole cherries at the bottom of the jar.

Grandma's lucky, I think to myself.

Grandma looks at my hands and says: Rake.

She pulls off her shirt.

Rake, she insists.

I put my warm hands to her velvet back and scratch.

She narrows her eyes and says: Rake, rake, harder, rake.

We only leave the veranda when a flash splits the sky. In a few days' time we'll be peeling today's sunshine off ourselves, it'll be coming off us in dry flakes. And that's when Ann's upper lip will harden and change into a scab.

REPTILE

The sun is making the earth crack. The plants lack moisture. The heatwave continues. All the rainwater barrels are empty. At daybreak I go with Grandpa to inspect the level of water in the well. I prise off the concrete cover with a crowbar.

Grandpa hisses.

I look down.

Around the well, most likely in its sleep, an adder has stretched out its zigzag-patterned body. My hands are shaking.

The adder raises its head and places it just above the low edge of the well, which has no casing.

One move and I could drop the cover on the reptile's head, I think.

I look at Grandpa, who's using a long twig to steer the snake's head into a hollow in the ground. He's trying to fit the pieces together like building bricks. Slowly I lower the cover.

Now, shouts Grandpa.

I pull out the crowbar.

*

We're sitting in silence on the stones on the boundary strip.

We deserve a cigarette, I say.

Yes, we do, he says.

HILL

It struck somewhere at the height of the nursery school, sparks ran along the high-tension wires, near the stream and the little chapel, the one that commemorates the boy, Maciek. About fifteen years ago he rode his new German motorbike under the wheels of a timber truck.

It was carrying beeches, so Grandpa said.

It struck hard, bloody hard, Ann reckons.

Danube won't brave the storm, he wants to sit it out. He's hiding in the wardrobe in the hall. He's buried himself in tablecloths and coverlets. He's groaning.

After the thunderclap the village is plunged in darkness. From the veranda I'm watching the way the glow-worms of lamps and candles pulsate within its fabric. It's time to feed the animals, so after their initial surprise that the electricity isn't back, the men come out of their houses. The lights of torches flash. The hillside opposite is twinkling.

Those people have returned to the hill. The postwoman told

us that over there they say the earth took its due, a sacrifice, Rybowicz, that it gorged itself, so now there'll be peace for a while.

I can see a swarm of human glow-worms. I imagine that from over there they must be seeing our hillside in a similar way. Flashes, glimmers, sparks.

Ann appears.

The animals are more alert when it's so very dark, I say.

And so are we, she says.

Soon we can hear the drawling voices of the animals from the slaughterhouse. Our cows join in with them.

They're singing, I say.

Yes, says Ann.

As the men from the other side of the hill finish work and enter their houses, we can see the light's intensity increasing in those interiors. I watch as the parish chairwoman's house brightens. I imagine everyone over there taking their places at tables covered with oilcloth in small kitchens painted a vivid lemon colour.

Fed and watered, the animals lay their heavy bodies on the straw, they exude heat, and the windowpanes in the stables are clouded by steam. The hens lower the membranes of their eyelids over their vigilant eyes.

Ann brings a candle onto the veranda.

This is from my first communion, she says, let's burn it.

The little tongue of fire that Ann kindles soon goes out.

In the west room the light of the consecrated candle works away on Grandma's face. She looks as if sculpted in marble.

*

Now the three of us are watching the opposite hillside through the window.

In this silence the slaughterhouse resounds. It's wheezing like a dying dog. The backup generators are starting to work. I imagine the workmen there returning to the procedures they carry out on animals that were interrupted by the darkness. Their bodies must have lost heat, they must have cooled down, and now, set in motion again, they're regaining temperature.

I'm imagining May, right now, from a bird's eye view. The borders of May are marked out by forests. May is dark, the hill-sides are bathed in night, with the sparks of lamps and candles glittering in it. In the middle, there it is, the slaughterhouse hill, illuminated by backup electricity, by light. And further off, if you look from a greater height, you can see the villages far away from May, with their backs turned on us, separated by the waters of the reservoir, by streams and forests. To the west Białe Gardła, to the east Wschód, beyond it Stary Sad. In every other direction forest.

The slaughterhouse is shining.

They know no rest there, they don't respect the night, says Grandma, and that's a sin.

HALL

Ever since the illness has taken up residence in this house, Grandpa devotes almost all his attention to the place. He occupies his hands with a petrol chainsaw, with floorboards, panelling, tiles.

Like this he's supporting life, not death, I think.

The professionals are coming, he says.

I've fixed the table saw, he says.

The cladding's coming, he says.

Grandpa mashes technical words in his mouth: mineral wool, PUR foam, radiator foil, putty, plexiglass.

It takes the workmen two days to tear off the old panelling in the hall and kitchen. Behind it we find insect nests and dead mice. We clean up.

When it's all done we sit beneath the walnut tree that great-grandfather Jan planted here in his youth.

The men offer us cigarettes. Grandpa fetches a honeycomb from the apiary, which he cuts up and shares among us. He puts a piece by for Grandma.

We chew the warm honeycomb.

Honey trickles down my gullet.

I mash sweetness in my mouth. I spit the sucked wax onto a saucer. I watch the men closely. It must be the first time they've ever seen a honeycomb. They put it in their mouths, break it into smaller pieces with their teeth and swallow. I don't say anything, because my curiosity takes the upper hand – I'm interested in seeing what this will do to them.

The roof, says Grandpa, pointing at the roof.

Grandpa persuades the men to take on another job.

The roof, we'll have to tear off the roof and put on a new one. Then we'll have to install central heating throughout the house, replace the windows with plastic ones, rip up the kitchen floorboards, put in a new bathtub, with the right kind of seat for Róża, and lay tiles too, white ones, he says.

The men say yes. The muscles of their bodies are gearing up for action. They're like Danube, I'm thinking, they're like our scent hound just before he sets off after a marten.

I look at Ann, who is gazing at one of them. He's similar to her, there's a similar brightness and beauty in them. I think they could make love beautifully, that he could fit close to her body beautifully, fill her up, and she could let a lot of things happen.

He's got up. Her eyes follow him. I see him approaching the gooseberry bush. I shift my gaze to Ann again, who doesn't take her eyes off him. Her face is twitching, something in it is smiling, but not her lips. She drops her gaze.

That night she tells me: I saw that man putting ripe gooseberries into his wide mouth with one hand, while shoving the other hand down his trousers, and then he slowly arranged his dick in a comfortable position.

EMPTY PLATES

They didn't leave any wax behind. Just empty plates. Licked clean. They must have swallowed it all, says Grandpa.

What will it do to them? I ask.

It's indigestible. If anyone were to tell them what they've eaten, it'd start to churn in their stomachs. If they don't find out, nothing will happen to them.

MOTION

That night we're woken by branches rapping against the windowpane. The wind has cooled the body of the house, and is working away in its bones. Grandma's illness is being quiet, allowing her to take steady, even steps. Remission sets her in motion. By the light of the full moon we're watching her slowly head towards the window.

She's like a plant attracted to the light. She's going to get proof of the light, I think.

Outside the window of the west room Grandpa has planted albizia, with flowers that shine at night.

Grandma has reached the window.

There are noises coming from the slaughterhouse.

Can you hear it, she asks.

Yes, we can, I reply.

The roots of the trees on this side are touching blood, says Grandma, it takes over their leaves.

The trees on the slaughterhouse side have shrunken leaves, necrotic stains instead of verdure. The squealing of pigs is the music of a great scream that not even the phloem of a larch tree can withstand, I think, and try to memorize it. I might make a poem out of it.

It causes illnesses to catch us, like the one that's working away in here, says Grandma, pointing at her distended belly. And like the one that's working away in the house – here she points at an efflorescence of fungus in the corner of the room. And like the one that takes over the leaves of plants – here she points at the shrivelled asparagus and fern.

May the whole world hear these sounds in their dreams, I say to Ann.

I say it as if I were uttering the words of a curse and the words of a prayer in the same breath.

I cover my head with a pillow and count to infinity.

MUZZLE

The wind is the song of the earth and it's entering the forest. The wind works away in the boughs of trees, it's warm and dry. If anyone runs across its path, it comes up to their eyes and fills their throats. It can't be breathed freely, it consumes all oxygen, although that's what it is, I'm thinking.

The wind mashes the forest.

I think of Rybowicz's cow, who found shelter with us and mashes so beautifully with her tongue, masticating the vetch.

The wind takes Ann's hair and rearranges it, plaiting and matting it. In the early autumn wind Ann is lovely, defenceless, pale.

The wind is the song of the earth, I say.

It's the spirit of the forest.

It's the conscience of the forest.

It's the circulatory system.

It's the litany.

It's scented.

It sings.

It darkens, says Ann.

The wind now drops, now rises from the trees.

Has the wind changed the course of the paths trodden by animals? asks Ann.

She doesn't trust the wind, she's heard frightful stories about it.

If the wind selects a victim it starts to blow in them, inside, she says.

Ann refuses to let the wind get inside her.

She's afraid.

I'm afraid, she says.

In her hand she has a plastic bottle full of birch water which has been dripping into it from a wound that Grandpa inflicted on the tree. I'll rub the birch water into the skin on Grandma's head.

More, Grandma will say.

All right, I'll answer.

But now we're in the forest. The wind comes up to us.

It's a strong beast, I'm thinking.

If you breathe in the wind the way you breathe in air, it'll blow inside you, says Ann, blocking my mouth with her hand. Don't inhale it. Follow the path trodden by the heifer, she issues an order, removes her hand and lets me breathe.

The wind is the song of the earth and it breaks the boughs of trees. Now the wind is like Danube scenting his way through the forest, now it's like the heifer waddling from the topmost fields towards the stable, I'm thinking.

The wind lies down with the night to sleep.

It closes its jaws.

It eases up.

We can see it coming from the trees at the northern edge of the forest, where it wags its birch-twig tail.

The wind and the night lie down to sleep in a dark hollow.

They scare a fox out of it.

In the moonlight Grandma wakes us standing by the window.

A fox has taken a hen from the stable and carried it into the forest, she says, somewhere out there in its den it's mincing white meat in its muzzle.

Grandma reacts to the wind like to insect bites, her skin itches from the wind, her legs swell up. I help her to get into bed. Watching has tired her, taking steps has tired her, breathing seems hard for her. I wait for her to fall asleep.

I'm falling asleep.

I have a dream: the wind, the night and the fox are strangling a hen and sharing it out between them.

In the morning, Grandma gazes at the forest from her bed.

The forest has turned its muzzle towards us today, she says.

Ann and I go into it. We search for mushrooms hidden under moss, we search for orange oak boletes and chanterelles.

Near the fox's den we find the damp traces of a fight.

HISS

We're emptying the kitchen. We carry out the chairs, the table, the kitchen cupboards. Finally we twist our spines beneath the weight of the sofa. We carry it behind the house, on the slaughterhouse side. We collapse in a heap.

None of this will ever go back into the kitchen, it'll all be new, it'll all be shiny, says Grandpa.

Through the window of the west room Grandma and Ann are watching us. They both have geranium leaves, crushed in my fingers, shoved deep into their ears. They're both complaining of pain. Grandma describes it as cold steel inserted through her ear into her head; Ann describes it as a hiss.

As if someone has put their cold lips to my ear and begun to hiss, she says, but the hiss has no way out, so it's growing in my head.

The wind, it's all the fault of the wind. While we were out on the veranda it was blowing treacherously, seeming pleasant, but getting cooler, prompting inflammation.

*

Tomorrow we'll rip up the kitchen floor, says Grandpa.

Yes, I say, yes.

MAW

Tomorrow Grandpa will open the maw and belly of the kitchen, I tell Ann as I use tweezers to pull out the geranium leaves that have been stuck in her ear for several hours.

Ow, she says, it's cold.

Under the kitchen floorboards there's everything, I say. All the gold and silver of my childhood, everything that passed through the narrow gap between the boards, an entire fortune.

In my hand I have some freshly picked geranium leaves. Grandma takes one of them and puts it in her mouth. Her gums mash the plant, her face twists, tenses, relaxes. Grandma spits out the chewed leaf. She rolls it into a ball and puts it in her other ear.

That ear too? I ask her.

My head is full of steel, here and here, she says, pointing at both ears, here and here, she repeats.

BELLY

Nothing in here will creak any more, says Grandpa.

I'm standing in the kitchen doorway, spying as the men from Stary Sad tear up the floorboards.

We fed the belly of this house throughout my childhood. The floor was well fed, sated, I'm thinking.

I'm looking at a narrow chink between the boards, through which we used to drop everything that was narrow, that sparkled and made a noise.

The men are ripping up those two boards.

Silver, gold, says one of them.

I step forward. I lean over and start to pick up the gold and silver of my childhood: coins brought via Silesia, Podlasie or Düsseldorf; medallions on which I read passages from prayers; devotional scapulars and little crosses from rosaries; needles and crochet hooks; gilt buttons.

I put it all in a small wooden casket that was once my mother's. Nothing is left in the belly of the house. The casket is full and its inside sparkles. I take it behind the house, to the spot where for years Grandpa has been burying dead animals. I use a spade to dig a small pit, I put the casket into the hole and bury it.

Grandma and Ann, who have geranium in their heads, who are full of geranium juice, are watching me through the window of the west room.

Didn't you want to show us? asks Ann when I go in to them.

It had to be buried quickly, it was a reminder of too much from the past, it would have distracted me from what's here and now, I say.

All the little crosses and all the medallions released from under the floor were singing, I think, but I keep that to myself.

EYES

We should give it a name of our own, I say to Ann.

Name it like a dog or like a heifer? she asks.

The name must be taken from a person. We should christen the illness, create good conditions for the illness, accept it, I say. It's a member of the family now. It should have a name that means something, that's associated with life, not death. We should talk to the illness, not forgetting the sick person as we talk. We should approach the illness, try to domesticate it. Give it a name. Yes, you're right, like for a dog. Just like for a dog.

Domesticate the illness? she asks.

Spin out the illness like a tale. Describe it, so there's life in it, I say. Feed it like an animal, without forgetting the sick person as we do so, but remembering that the illness and Grandma are not one thing. The illness is, let's imagine, a bracket fungus that has overgrown this house.

And what if we give it the name of a dead person? she asks.

An illness can't bear death, that's its end, I persuade her.

I have trust in what I'm saying. I examine what I've articulated, I'm surprised by the forthright nature of my judgements, but I carry on: If you call the illness by the name of a dead person it'll rise to Grandma's throat. It'll take revenge. The illness has something of a betrayed woman about it. The illness won't forgive, it won't back off. If the ailing body trembles, is afraid, it feels at home inside it. And it grows. The illness can't bear competition, if it grows, it occupies everything around it: the plants, the walls of the house, the thick winter overcoats. Look what's happening to the plants, look how they're weakening in Grandma's room, first the aloe, then the fern, and now the geranium. Only the animals seem beyond it. You see how Azrael kneads Grandma's belly? He does it tenderly, in that spot the illness emits heat, so the cat gains from it.

Does that help her? she asks.

Nothing helps her. Grandma's illness, I say, is like a bird, that well-fed rooster who strolls beneath the veranda.

Donchiquito, yes? she asks.

Donchiquito, yes, I say.

Those are the same eyes. The illness and Donchiquito are alike. Look in his eyes one day. When Grandma's eyes start to resemble Donchiquito's golden-hazel eyes that'll be the end.

I'd love to give it a name taken from a curse, she says.

Don't call out the name from a curse, I tell her, a name like that will return, it'll occupy your belly or your chest. It'll blossom.

PULSE

Low down on her belly Grandma has an elongated scar. I know my mother came from there. My source springs from there too.

Whenever I run a sponge over the scar, Grandma says: First they pulled out your aunt. I knew it was imminent. The animals never took their eyes off me. They watched. As if they could sense it. Can you imagine that? A month before the due date. I didn't know how many of those children there were. Two of them. First they pulled out your aunt; she was big and strong, she had thick skin. I could breathe freely. But I could tell they hadn't pulled everything out of me. The parish chairwoman's mother, who was poking around in me, shouted: There's another. She put her hands in me. It was a mess down there: blood and everything that comes from a person. And out of it they pulled your mother – parchment, not skin, rivers of veins. Then they took us to the hospital because there were complications.

Grandma is inspecting me.

And here, look, she says, pointing a wet hand at the pulsating vein on my temple. Your mother had a vein like that here and you've got one too. Just here, she says.

That day, at the hospital, when they took her away from me for ages, Grandma continues, it occurred to me that I'd recognize her by the vein working away on her temple. And look, after all these years, decades on, I'm able to recognize her in you by exactly that.

BOUNDARY STRIP

The boundary strip is coated in blood. A September storm is carrying the redness on, down the village, into river after river. Some of it will reach the sea to the north, I'm thinking.

It will take revenge, says Grandma.

Today she hasn't taken a single step, today she only wants frigid Scandinavian poems.

I read, taking the words from Ekelöf: 'Yes, to be one with the night, one with myself, with the candle's flame / which looks me in the eye still, unfathomable and still, / one with the aspen that trembles and whispers, / one with the crowds of flowers leaning out of darkness to listen to something I had on my tongue to say but never said, / something I don't want to reveal even if I could. / And that it murmurs inside me of purest happiness! / And the flame rises... It is as though the flowers crowded nearer, / nearer and nearer the light in a rainbow of shimmering points. / The aspen trembles and plays, the evening red passes / and all that was inexpressible and distant is inexpressible and near.'

*

The IV drip is working away, I've hung it up level with a holy picture, in which Roch is showing the wound on his thigh.

I imagine the stuff in the drip must be sweet.

You're feeding the illness, not me, says Grandma.

We're feeding life, I say.

Bloody hell, I think.

The stream fuelled by the blood of animals attracts insects, the storm was short enough for the water not to be moving violently. It's trickling through the stones, through the roots of elm trees. Level with the church, at the point where the stream slows down, the blood spreads, so I imagine, just as usual, in the dam built by the Swarts.

The valley stinks.

Let there be a great flood, says Grandma.

I can see flashes of lightning illuminating the dark sky above the Upper Forest. Is the storm moving west, will it rinse out the vein of the stream?

The cows we're driving from the meadows on the other side of the stream won't plunge their muzzles in the water. They can smell the blood.

It's the blood of cows, I'm thinking.

We're standing in the current. Ann is wearing a yellow cape and green rubber boots. I'm in a red anorak that lets the rain through and identical rubber boots.

All this colour, says Ann, casting a glance at our stylized shepherdess outfits.

We're quite simply the Vogue models of the village, I quip.

I call the dog. As I noticed before going to fetch the cows, Danube has buried himself in the barn, in the hay. But now he has recognized the passing of the storm and my whistle. I can hear him approaching the stream, there's an attendant whimper.

The cows cross the stream and at the edge of it they shake themselves.

They're disgusted by us, says Ann.

SHAWL

Night, Grandma asks for the silk shawl that's hanging over her woollen coat. It's her going-out costume. She wants to be buried in it.

Silk is like the body of the stream, cool, slowly trickling down the village.

Once, animals were drowned in it, small pests, yes, the water accepts everything, she says, smoothing the shawl.

Night. A storm, the second today, comes from the direction of the reservoir, and strikes at the top of the village. May's land is lit up by lightning. This time Danube has hidden among the cows. I gaze at those great bodies and that quivering dog. Their strength calms him, he's falling asleep among them. The body parts are mixed up here: a dog's head, soft udders, horns, warm muzzles. Rybowicz's cow has her eyes open. Her wounds are healing. She likes to be near the other cows. At night her muzzle must touch another muzzle.

The water is moving. The cold batters the windowpanes. After a time the water in the stream is running pure again.

When the clouds give way to the new moon a concert begins, the pigs delivered to the slaughterhouse are squealing. Soon, along with the next storm, their blood will go into the elms.

The elm trees here are dwarfish, stooping.

A plant that feeds on the blood of an animal weakens, says Grandma.

Let all this be just a dream, says Ann.

SONG

Get up and walk, I hear Grandma's voice, as if in my sleep.

Jesus, I think.

I open my eyes. In the darkness of the room I can see the stain of Grandma's body, she's leaning over me, the skin of her hand is cold.

Get up and walk, she repeats.

Jesus, I say.

I call myself to order.

Calm down, I think. It's just Grandma who's got up, and is walking, and is telling me: Get up and walk.

I get up and walk.

The stain of Grandma's body leads me to the veranda.

Listen, she tells me.

I'm listening, I say.

And I listen.

The slaughterhouse is singing, singing, she says.

*

Only at dawn do I think of a miracle – Grandma couldn't walk, but she got up and walked, was she really moving, or was I merely dreaming?

DAMP

I'm standing before the mirror. It has been here for years. The wooden frame is unfit for the damp bathroom. The varnish is peeling, the wood is losing its gloss, cracking, delaminating. Moments ago I was touching Grandma's body here, it's more and more immune to the rough strokes of the horsehair brush. Grandma is like an animal that needs to be scratched on its body, especially its back. Grandma wants it done harder, for longer.

At these times she arches her spine and says: Rake.

My grandma is like an animal, I think.

My hands and wrists ache from scratching. My fingertips are wrinkled from the warm water. I won't let them return to a normal state for ages. But before immersing my body in the water, which I sprinkle with Bochnia salt tinted green and scented like a pine forest, I touch myself.

Breasts. I stroke them like an expert, I know how I ought to feel them under my fingers. I imagine that Ann does the same, that my mother did the same, that all the women in this valley and all the women beyond this valley have stood, are standing and will stand before the mirror at night when their warm houses are already going to sleep. Examining their bodies.

I look at my left breast, which has always been noticeably larger. Some fifteen years ago I found a tick embedded there. Its dark abdomen was impossible to grip between my fingernails, it was soft and slippery. And then my heart began to work away in my belly, beating hard and rapidly. The alien thing in my body forced me to vomit. My fingers were trembling, but not badly enough to stop me from using the nail clippers. Along with the arachnid I cut out a little chunk of flesh. It left a dent, now healed into a scar. I doused it in propolis tincture. It burnt.

Grandpa calls it a question of blood, this tendency of ours to be tick feeders. The ticks and mosquitoes leave Grandma in peace.

Just the nipple and the armpits to go.

Clean.

I get into the bathtub and immerse my body in water.

The handle tilts towards the floor. Ann opens the door. She doesn't knock. Ever since Grandma fell ill, no one knocks in this house. The illness has opened all the doors.

Anyone can enter any room, there's no place for intimacy, we can't afford it here.

Everything is out on display.

Everything watches everything.

Everything looks at everything.

Everything has become communal.

There's a scent of forest, says Ann.

Yes, I say.

Let's set fire to it, she says and takes out a cigarette.

She sits on the floor, leans her back against the bath, and her head is within my reach. She tilts it back. She closes her eyes. She's beautiful. She's been carrying the cigarette around with her all day in her shirt pocket. She lights it, takes a drag and hands it to me ceremonially, as if passing me the Host.

Burning the illness, I say, take a drag and immerse my body in the water.

Only the hand holding the cigarette is still sticking out of it. After a while I can feel Ann taking it off me. I squeeze my eyelids, in my head I can feel rising pressure, I'm starting to lack oxygen, the cigarette smoke is dissolving in my lungs.

I surface.

Ann hands me the Klub.

Are you afraid? she asks.

No, I reply. I take a drag, it gives me an alibi.

I immerse myself in the water and there, beneath the surface, I think how I'd like her hands to hold my head under water. And not let go.

ORANGES

Night comes up to the windows.

The body of the night is damp. The night is eyes. It's gazing at us.

The night is panting like a dog, says Grandma.

The night is panting like a dog, repeats Ann.

A week ago Grandma lay down in bed and since that time she hasn't raised her body again.

Get up, I say to her.

I haven't any muscles, she replies. Ever since I've been unable to swallow the meat of large animals I've been shrinking. Switch off the light, please.

I switch it off and go out into the hall. I take a felt-tip pen and a yellow notebook with me. I write something down that might be fit for a poem: In several hours the moon will enter the body of the night.

I go back and settle down beside Ann.

I fall asleep.

At night I hear Grandma's voice.

Show me how to place my feet, she whispers.

It only took a week, I think, for her body to forget basic movements, for something in her muscles to slacken.

Grandma raises her head from the pillow.

Teach me to walk, she says.

Moonlight illuminates the floorboards. The Canary Island ivy winding above the holy pictures is watching as we lead Grandma along.

She doesn't weigh a thing.

We lead her fragile bones across the room.

Meanwhile I forget to breathe. Leading Grandma's bones across the creaking floorboards parches my throat.

The night, which is eyes, is watching this scene inside the house, the house that in a while Grandpa is going to cover with white cladding and arm with radiator ribs.

After completing one length of the room Grandma says: Enough.

We escort her back to the bed, we lie her down on it and cover her with the eiderdown.

She falls asleep.

At dawn she wakes up and wakes us with a cough.

Sometimes I dream, she says, that I get out of bed and walk into the forest. And I don't think about how to place my feet to avoid falling over. I walk. I think about the herbs, whether I'll still find them in the same places. And when in my dream I touch the geum flowers, the pain wakes me up.

From lying down her skin is starting to look like orange peel. But her body doesn't smell of fruit. It smells of Sudocrem, talc, urine and shit. Our hands smell of Sudocrem, talc, urine and shit, but also of the oranges we peel for her each morning. The oranges stick in her throat. But she asks for them.

What sort of a grandma has to be fed like a child, she says. Like that, she's unfit to be a grandma. She can't be a substitute mother any more.

Her pupils are dilating.

WHITE MEAT

Tell a story, Ann asks me that night. A fable to send us to sleep.

I tell her this: The night is eyes and ears. The night is capable of watching and listening, but this engenders no feelings in it. The night is attentive to sounds and images, at the same time it's a creature that buries sounds and images near the fox's den, we mustn't forget that the fox is not at the service of the night.

What about the fox? asks Ann.

The fox must change his den every night. Soon the entire topmost forest will be full of fox dens, I say. The fox likes white meat, the fox is grateful for white meat, white meat makes his body stronger. At night the nimble body of the fox can be seen in the village – he knows the valley farms meat for him. The white meat of a single bird can occupy his stomach for several days. The night is a creature similar to a fox. Once, I dreamt that a vixen had young with the night. They were exquisite, with copper-coloured fur, but they had no eyes or ears, although in the dream I knew they were pure watching and listening, I say. The night is fertile, I say, looking at the new moon outside.

Young with the night? asks Ann in a whisper.

At dawn the night returns to the den, I say, there it lies down beside the vixen, and covers her with its great body. They copulate. Their young are born after two months. This offspring of the night and the vixen are recognizable by the fact that the young like to play with the feathers of Sebright hens carried off to the den. And Sebright feathers are beautiful, as if painted with eyeliner.

AGAVE

The one about the agave, asks Grandma.

I start: 'The agave lives three hundred years. It lives very long because it cannot walk – which means it can't meet any other agave.'

Once again, asks Grandma.

I read: 'The agave lives three hundred years. It lives very long because it cannot walk – which means it can't meet any other agave.'

Again, asks Grandma.

I close my eyes, drive my fingernails into the skin of my forearm and say, from memory now: 'The agave lives three hundred years. It lives very long because it cannot walk – which means it can't meet any other agave.'

Three hundred years, repeats Grandma. Can you imagine?

Three hundred, she whispers.

FLAMES

Days of remission are followed by collapse again. I enter Grandma's bed as if I'm entering a fox's den. My body is able to give off warmth.

The house is making noises: it creaks inside like a tree whipped by the wind, and on top of that sounds from the forest and the slaughterhouse resonate clearly.

I think of the pictures that hang on opposite walls of the west room. Our Lady on the northern wall and Jesus on the southern. Grandma likes to choose between them. One day she says: I'd rather Mary. Another day she says: I'd rather Jesus. She doesn't explain her choices, out of faith she chooses whichever she happens to need.

Following remission, the cold gives Grandma a hard time. Grandma has her mouth slightly open, through the parchment of her skin one can study her veins.

Following days of remission there's anxiety that one day, maybe soon, this will end, but also anxiety that it will go on eternally.

*

I go out onto the veranda and light a Klub. Between drags I say: The illness is like an obscenity and like a blessing.

VIXEN

So it's death, Vixen, I say to the body of an animal drowned in the stream. She must have fallen from the bluff, she must have plunged her muzzle in the water and drawn the wet into her lungs.

Oh Vixen, I say, now who's going to bark in the stream? Who's going to creep up to the henhouses in the valley? Who's going to bring fox cubs into the world? What about the white meat the village has farmed for you? Oh Vixen, what shall I tell Grandma? That death has taken you? I can't say that, bringing news of a loss into the house is forbidden. Oh Vixen, what's to be done with your body?

Branches have trapped the fox's body. Water is slowly pulling off the skin, which will drift down the village, leaving the bones here, perhaps.

Don't worry, Vixen, when it's time, I'll come and bury your remains.

I promise.

HUNGER

I am older than Grandma, though the hands she folds to pray testify to something else.

I am older than Grandma, I say to Ann, who's bringing in fir wood for kindling.

Yes, she says, for she has no objection in her.

Grandma is like a child in the fog. Today I prayed for her death. For death for her, I say.

So did I, says Ann.

Our prayers are nasty, I say.

Nasty, she repeats.

Ann is beautiful, as she says it the scar on her right cheek pulses in concert with her heartbeats.

Lately I dreamt there are two hearts working away in Ann, one of which she'll give away to something that will creep up to a house in the valley at night. This something will be carrying one of Ann's hearts in its muzzle and will feed its young with it.

I think she must still have those two hearts inside her, because only then is it possible to pray for death as if also sensing that this means life.

CALADIUM

The araucaria has stabbed its roots through the plastic flower pot.

Life, says Grandma, and asks to be brought dark earth from near the apiary.

I replant the araucaria in the cool November sun. Just a few weeks on it's starting to lose its needles and droop towards the ground.

At night I'm woken by quiet steps, Grandma's body has gained strength again, she's wandering from the leggy begonia to the caladium with leaves as if made of paper with dark green nerves running through them, and on to the west-facing window that overlooks the slaughterhouse, where she stops beside the dracaena. I know that the low temperature in the west room irritates this subtropical plant, but I haven't moved it into the east room.

After Grandma got her diagnosis we moved all the flowers into the west room. They were to retain the moisture, to be a reminder of nascent life, and to wrangle with loss. But loss has been taking over their delicate structures, starting with the leaves or the roots.

In late November I discover sticky mealy bugs on the leaves of the croton. Grandma's hands wipe the leaves with soapy water and alcohol by turns. And although Grandma fights against loss by destroying the bugs, from time to time she looks up from the plant and says: Taking life to hold on to life.

On the day when it first snows Grandma must own up to loss.

So it's death, she says, and points out the spot where I'm to bury the plant.

Kuba is already lying here, the Weimaraner. Nero is here too, the German shepherd hit by a car outside the Wilks' house, where there's still a bloodstain on the asphalt to this day. His death spilt out in the shape of Japan. Krat is lying here too. Equipped with a burin, Grandma's hands have etched all these names on a nearby stone.

We bury the plants in the earth, which is frost-bound.

Should we say the Eternal Rest for plants? asks Ann.

Yes, I reply, touching her cheek, pink from the cold, as I say it.

In a whisper I utter the words of the prayer: Eternal blossoming grant unto them, O Lord.

Our hands are ossifying from working in the cold ground.

We're feeding the earth with plants, whispers Ann.

When it's all over we stick out our warm tongues and catch geometric snowflakes on them.

In the window of the west room I spot Grandma. Now it's plain to see how much she has dwindled since the summer. From time to time steam from her mouth settles on the windowpane.

Life, in spite of all, I say into the cold.

TOPS

She is like a bird, especially now, on the threshold of winter. The illness has taken Grandma in its grip again, it won't let her walk. Our days, mine and my women's, are leaning more and more heavily towards the night, we wake close to noon, we lay down our tired bodies after midnight. In ever weaker daylight we make fragrant meals, all from vegetables picked this autumn in the field: peppers, yellow courgettes, musky pumpkins, red potatoes. Added to that, spices brought by Ann from distant Asia. Grandma likes to sniff and identify the flavours.

Evening conversations on the veranda aren't possible any more, in the light of a sparkling fluorescent lamp. Our place has been taken over by the cold. Ann and I sit in the west room, leaning our backs against the stove. The radiator ribs are still lying in the hall.

We tell stories, that's how we power life.

OUR LADY

The house is ill. The body of the house is like the body of a sick person. The hunger of these walls in winter is unbearable. The hunger of the house comes from the cold. In this house the stove must be lit long before dawn. Early in the morning Grandpa starts feeding it with fire. Otherwise the bones of the house will be chilly. It's best not to let them cool down entirely.

The house is ill and I'm not sure whose illness came first: Grandma's or the house's.

We move around it cautiously, we don't want to wake Grandma. I imagine that viewed from the height of the apiary it looks like a sleeping animal sprawling in the rose bushes and the boughs of the walnut trees.

The heart of the house is the little shrine: a patched-up plaster Our Lady, as I call her, two little blue vases, empty in winter, an embroidered doily and a little metal cross, which during his Christmas pastoral visit the parish priest puts to our burning lips. I kiss it, because I still can't not do it. There's metal and rust.

Fungus has been flourishing since summer in a corner of the west room. Its bloom is stretching towards the leggy fern.

It's growing and climbing like the ivy, says Grandma.

Grandpa is setting procedures in motion, he's going to heal this room.

I'll take care of it, I'll bring in the professionals, he says.

We move Grandma into the east room.

Grandma's bones are cold.

Grandma's skin is cold.

It's no good, the damp follows me, she says, touching a pink wall of the east room, behind which the heated lungs of the kitchen stove are working away.

THE COLD

It's hungry, I say to Ann.

Yes, she says.

Eat, croaks Grandma.

Winter has entered May, large and soft. May is slowing down its activities. The residents of May are pressing their heads to windowpanes coated in flowers of frost and saying: The whole of May is covered in snow.

May's asphalt has vanished under snow.

Pheasants are emerging from the birch groves.

May is cut off from the world, I'm thinking.

Eat, croaks Grandma.

What would you like? I ask.

Red stuff, croaks Grandma.

In summer I froze some strawberries. I was already thinking of the monotony of winter, of the cold, and also of the illness, which would have to be fed.

I go up to the fridge, bend over and open the freezer door. I fetch out the strawberries and tip them into a bowl.

I bend over again. There's curiosity in me. I take a look at Grandpa's stores. They seem to have been lying here for years on end. The bodies of birds tightly fill two whole drawers. I recognize the skin of turkeys and the skin of ducks. My attention is caught by the topmost drawer, the narrowest. I slide it open. Rows of used matchboxes line the bottom of it. On each one I can see a date – a year. They're also marked with small coloured dots and heavenly landscapes sketched in pen.

I pick up one of the boxes, the striking strip is unscratched. I push the little drawer with a finger.

There she is.

It's a bee mother.

I open another box – and there's another, in another – another, in another – another. And so on.

The lifeless, frozen mother bees vary in the colour of the spots on their backs.

Queen marking, I whisper.

A childhood memory returns of Grandpa letting me mark the backs of the bee mothers, each year in a different colour.

So this is where you bury them. This is a vast graveyard. Grandpa's great humanitarian gesture – to take life in a way that's like laying to rest, I think.

I cover my tracks. I put the boxes back in their places.

I use the strawberries to make a warm mousse with an added spoonful of dandelion honey.

It's sweet, says Grandma.

She mashes the red stuff in her mouth, she mashes away and it looks endless.

GOLD

There's no one to decorate the gold altars, says Grandma. There's no one to bring flowers. There's no one to deck the tall Christmas trees in December. And ever since they've been artificial, the Christmas trees go high, high, almost halfway up the main altar. One year in December, about ten years ago, some women from the village came to see me, and one of them, the one who sews, said: Róża, your granddaughter hasn't got a husband, as you know, all the unmarried girls are to do the decorations. Have her come on the first Saturday in December. We must adorn the church, deck the Christmas trees, wash the floors. To which I told them that my granddaughter, that you are out in the world. Bring her, one of them told me, the other one, who serves at the presbytery. I told them that my granddaughter is married to the world, that's what I told them, and I added that she no longer belongs to us. They backed off and left the hall. I probably hurt their feelings, but nobody's going to give orders to the women of this house.

You told them the right thing, says Ann, and strokes her hands.

That's nice: She's married to the world, I'll have that for a poem, I say to Grandma.

Have it, have it, she says, have it.

At night I think about the fact that indeed, it's the virgins who hang the large, bald heads of golden baubles on the artificial Christmas trees.

Pure hands.

Untouched bodies.

Throats – narrow and pure.

BONES

Why do so many wild animal bones end up in the stream? I ask Grandpa as he treats me to a cigarette on the veranda.

Well, he begins, the smarter ones chase the stronger ones into the stream. The wolves know how to do it. When it's slippery and wet they have an advantage. They know how to chase a large stag into a trap, they lead it to the edge of the bluff, and any body as big as that will fall off it. I've seen their prey in the stream more than once. The wolves take what's theirs, and then the hunters come along and take everything else. Once, when I was a small boy, I found the body of a stag in the upper course of the stream. The wolves had hounded it to death, or else dogs did it. The stream parted on either side of it, because that huge body created a dam. The hunters were quicker than the animals, they turned up on time, at a good moment, when the wild had killed the wild. They chopped off the head with the antlers. God knows why they left the rest. A stag with no head and antlers is an ugly sight.

It's hard to imagine anything like it, I say. What did you do with the body? I ask.

I always leave the wild to the wild, he says.

FIRE

The winter makes Grandma's eyes look as if they're made of glass. It's hard for her to keep them fixed on anything. Her gaze slides across the whiteness beyond the window. It finds nothing to latch on to. It slides across the whiteness of the room. It latches on to the pink of a flowering Christmas cactus, stops on the green of a philodendron guided along twine hung from the ceiling.

My eyesight needs greenery, says Grandma.

I remember a winter like this one in my early childhood. At the time, we children were pushed outdoors to harden our bodies. We came home with reddened cheeks and fingers which as soon as they regained warmth began to burn, to sting. The smarting released a prolonged moan from our throats that changed into weeping.

We haven't had a winter like this one for a very long time, says Grandma.

Ever since the heavy snow came to the village, the body of the valley has been slumbering. Only the slaughterhouse hill is in motion. On the surface of the snow there are visible fractures, dislocations, dark fissures.

It's in motion. Soon it will all move downwards, the hill will touch the stream with its great tongue, I tell Ann.

Yes, she says.

We're waiting.

BULLFINCH

The winter demands that we keep the fire going in the cast-iron stove. There hasn't been time to install the radiator ribs yet.

I like to keep the fire going, to incite warmth, in this illness I like to occupy my hands with something. The dry branches surrender to my touch, and at these moments I know this will result in heat for my ailing grandma.

This morning I'm putting dried Christmas tree branches into the stove. Grandpa is in the habit of killing a young tree each year. He does it for the fragrance. He wants the tree to bear the weight of the glitter-speckled baubles and to shine with angel hair. But later on, as soon as the priest's pastoral visit is over, he crams it into the storage space and waits a year for it to dry out. After a year he assigns it the role of tinder.

I break off a twig and lay the kindling.

As I'm setting fire to it Grandma asks me a question.

What sort of bird is that, over there, outside? she says.

I go up to the curtain and look.

A bullfinch, I say.

Read to me about the bullfinch, she says.

I open the guide and search for it.

I summarize the bit about the sound, Grandma likes those bits: It produces a short whistle or fluted note, 'phü', with a melancholy ring, locally in Europe with a distinctly falling pitch, 'pyüüuh'.

Phü-pyuuu, I force out of myself.

Pfiyuuu, repeats Grandma.

I look at the beak she makes while imitating the bullfinch.

It's cold, she says suddenly, as if she's just remembered about the cold weather.

I put down the book and go up to the stove.

It's going shaaaa.

I open the little door.

Now I know.

I've ignited hell.

Air feeds the flames. I feel a brush of fire on my face. It lasts a split second. My body doesn't act fast enough to dodge it. I can smell burning hair. The thought crosses my mind that it smells like the singed skin of the pigs that the butcher up by the reservoir used to flay every Easter.

I touch my face.

Grandma is watching.

Pfiyu, pfiyu, she says, as if she has adopted the language of a songbird.

Show me, she says.

I go up to her.

Grandma, in whom the morphine is starting to take effect, touches my face, just as the blind touch the faces of strangers, that's to say, sensitively.

You're like porcelain, she says.

Under her fingertips I can feel that I've lost my eyelashes.

You've lost your lashes, she says.

She passes me a damp handkerchief wetted with aloe vera juice. I associate the scent of it with Grandma, with the crannies of her body to which I apply it so that she'll smell nice. Grandma is soon tired by her efforts to treat me. She lies down and after a few deep breaths she falls asleep.

A couple of days later the redness on my face disappears and my skin recovers its normal shade. Each evening I check in the mirror to see how my lashes are doing.

I look at Ann's long eyelashes. They're beautiful.

After a few days I get used to not having any.

How fortunate it is that I don't have to please anyone, just the illness, but it loves everything, I think. I keep guard in Grandma's room, I'm like a dog.

I won't be showing my body to any outsiders this winter.

I only remember about my eyelashes once they're long enough for it to be impossible to tell if they're different from before.

On the night when I realize they've grown back, I dream about Grandma. In the dream the chemo has occupied her hair; in the dream we comb it in turn, first me, then Ann. Each stroke of the brush makes a tangle of the grey hair that's left on her. In this dream Grandma loses her eyebrows and eyelashes.

Her face is as white as snow, with deeper wrinkles than outside the dream, and more sharply defined freckles.

As well as the illness there's life going on inside her, I think in this dream.

On awakening I see her with the brush in her hand. She has managed to undo the plait braided by Ann a few days ago, but she has only had enough strength in her hands for a few brush strokes.

Take this and plait it, she says.

I brush her hair.

Show me the brush, she says.

It's clean, the strokes haven't removed any hair.

Not just yet, I think to myself.

Go on brushing, she says.

I brush her hair and plait it. The plait is thin, like a mouse's tail.

Give it to me, she says and points at my hair.

I stoop enough for her not to have to raise her hands high. She sets her knees apart, and I move into the space from which my mother emerged. Grandma takes my hair in her hands and plaits it. She does it slowly, with effort.

We're close.

Grandma makes the loveliest plaits, I think.

Is the earth underneath the slaughterhouse moving? she asks after a long silence.

Yes, I reply.

Then it'll move downhill in the spring, she says.

CHRISTMAS EVE

The one about animals, says Grandma.

I begin: 'Faithful creatures hacked to death / foundered horse cow dog / come to me embrace me / kiss on the lips on the brow on the lips.'

Once again, says Grandma.

I whisper: 'Faithful creatures hacked to death / foundered horse cow dog / come to me embrace me / kiss on the lips on the brow on the lips.'

Again, she says.

I whisper: 'Come to me embrace me.'

I look at her now sleeping body.

I kiss Grandma on her chapped lips.

I put out the light.

Soon after, the horses of silver cars head down the asphalt to midnight Mass.

SHIELDING

It starts with earache. I know they'll have to separate us. My illness cannot come into conflict with her illness. My weakness cannot affect her body.

We must care for the purity of our illnesses. Singly there's nobility in them, something that allows them to be described, to be classified, to be advised on, I'm thinking.

I move into the east room.

I share it with Grandpa.

An infection of the upper airways and an inflammation of the inner ear are the last thing I should share with Grandma. My own illness frustrates me: heavy head, darkness before my eyes, something sleepless in me.

The separation unsettles me, though we're only divided by a couple of walls and the hall.

I want to go to that death, I say to Ann in my fever.

Hey, she scolds me.

I ring Grandma and ask about her night, I ask about her day, I read her lines from a poem by Czesław Miłosz: 'Riding birds, feeling under our thighs the soft feathers / Of goldfinches, orioles, kingfishers, / Or spurring lions into a run, unicorns, leopards, / Whose coats brush against our nakedness, / We circle the vivid and abundant waters—'

Ann comes in and interrupts me.

Grandma has fallen asleep, the phone has dropped onto her pillow. You were reading to her dream, she says.

Ann attends to us. She's calm and careful. She's beautiful as she hands me hot mallow tea. Ann keeps an eye on the times when I'm to take shielding pills and an antibiotic. It starts to work away in me unquickly. Ann is beautiful at the moments when she takes our illnesses into her mouth and talks of them as being temporary, as something to wait out in bed, for which a remedy exists.

My illness frustrates me. It's taking away my days with Grandma, but it also allows me to rest, my hands stop smelling of Grandma's body, her skin, her fluids.

The space in the east room irritates me, the noise of the television, the smell of Sudocrem that Ann brings on her hands from Grandma's room. Grandpa has become even quieter, he's embarrassed, he has unlearnt intimacy.

I want to go to her, I say to Ann in my fever.

Hey, she scolds me again.

Ten days later I've recovered. I go to Grandma's room. I'm amazed by how efficient her illness is, that it only needed a few days to take away so much of her body.

You're looking beautiful, I lie.

Lying to the sick is justified, I think. Every physical change in Grandma seems to be the last. We cannot imagine any more, we cannot allow any more.

The illness is a cunning mistress, it works away slowly, scrupulously, during the day it distracts our attention from the surgical incisions in the patient's body. It undoubtedly quickens its activity during the night. The changes are so subtle that you can only observe them from the perspective of several days' separation, because if you're at the patient's side day after day, hour after hour, there's a blindness inside you that must stem from a faith in life. I think about this at length on a snowy night.

PRIORITY

Grandpa avoids Grandma's illness, any ceremony around illness is alien to him, he refuses to know anything about illness, or to touch anything that's ill, but I can see that he's watching Grandma through the veranda window. He's smoking a Klub.

At daybreak he tells me about his dream.

Since the illness took up residence in our house, I dream of animals stricken by rabies, he says. I dream of dogs digging holes beneath the gooseberry bush and laying their bodies down in them.

Yes, I say.

We're all sick, the illness turns all our stomachs, I'm thinking.

Grandma isn't opening her eyes. We can hear her body working away. We feed it through the drip, and take care of the morphine patches. That evening Ann and I decide I'll sleep beside her.

No, Grandpa protests, I'll be beside her.

I yield this priority to him.

That night, by the light of the headlamps, I spy on them.

They're dovetailed. Grandpa is pressing his lips against Grandma's back and breathing into it, just as if he were blowing air into her. It's the first time I've ever seen such intimacy between them.

What does it portend? I wonder.

FIRE SALAMANDER

I'm here, just as I promised, Vixen, I say to the animal's bones.

The water has done its job. It has cleaned the bones of meat and sticky tissues. The stream has polished what was left. I pick up the spine. I rattle it. I pick up the tibias, which have sunk to the bottom of the stream. I strike one against the other. Calm today, the sheet of water carries the sound onwards, down the village.

Your bones emit low tones, Vixen, your singing is low, Vixen, I say.

I extract the little skull that's wedged between some rocks. It's like porcelain. Not a single tooth is missing.

Everything in you is symmetrical, precise, exact, I say to the skull.

I gather the remaining bones. They're light. I carry them uphill, towards a blackthorn bush, above the bluff, from which the animal must have fallen. I dig a pit with a shovel that belongs to Grandpa, I brought it with me.

I want something from you, Vixen, I say to the remains. I break a piece of mandible off the rest of the skull.

Snap.

The earth is sympathetic. January has brought warmth.

I feel a trickle of sweat between my breasts.

I toss the vixen's white bones into the open pit. I say a prayer over them, which feels like blasphemy.

I'll always have rituals, ceremonies inside me, I think.

I fill in the pit and lay a stone on top, untidily, in the language of chaos. I sit down beside it, fetch out the snapped-off piece of mandible and put it to my lips.

I'll blow into you, Vixen, I say, and blow.

Soon I'm out of breath.

Blowing into you, Vixen, sparking a song from you is a hard task, I say to the grave.

I lie down on it and watch the clouds being driven by the wind. After a while I can feel something climbing up my skin in the wrist area. A fire salamander takes a step and stops, tickles my skin, takes a step and freezes. I spot three more, coming from the direction of the beech trees, moving towards the vixen's grave. The sun has woken them a few months too early.

Poor things, I think, there's still more snow to come.

I get up and walk away.

Here are the mourners, I think, come to lament over the bones of their forest sister.

At home, before entering Grandma's room, I scrub my hands.

You smell of earth, she says, while I'm changing her morphine patch.

She grabs me by the hands and sniffs them.

WHITE

Vixen, the village knew you went in for white. Grandpa figured out your weakness, he didn't object to it, he fed it.

At the farms in the village there wasn't much white to be found, and anything white was for you. Everyone knew that you only dragged the white from the henhouses.

At the fair the villagers superstitiously bought hens that were deep rust or black in colour. If something white was born, they left one, and swapped the rest with Grandpa for another colour. Hen for hen, rooster for rooster, pigeon for pigeon, rabbit for rabbit.

While you were alive, here, by the forest, in the valley, white meant death, but Grandpa didn't object to it. Through you, Vixen, he fed it.

WARM

Grandpa avoids Grandma's illness, any ceremony around illness is alien to him, he refuses to know anything about illness, or to touch anything that's ill, but he wants a warm house for Grandma, and that occupies his thoughts.

He's feeding the house's illness, I say to Ann.

Yes, she says.

We're losing the forests and arable fields, building plots and birch groves, and also the grazing land. People have been coming to us from the city, men who talk beautifully and correctly.

They've caught wind of loss.

They've caught wind of weakness.

They've caught wind of need.

Grandpa doesn't tell me about the details, or the deals he makes with these people. Only this: It's all for Grandma.

After a while I find some documents that talk about selling the forests, arable fields, building plots, birch groves and grazing land.

Grandpa is swapping our forests for polystyrene.

It must be warm for Grandma, he says.
Grandpa is swapping the building plots for a furnace.
It must be warm for Grandma, he says.
Grandpa is swapping the grazing land for plastic windows.
It must be warm for Grandma, he says.

LEGACY

I'm walking into the forest with Ann and Danube.

I'm telling a tale: Choose, said Grandpa over twenty years ago, pointing at these fields, at the hilltops. I was up on the rack wagon, treading down the hay he'd put in it. I was to choose the plot where I'd build a house when I grew up. Without a second thought I chose this one here, on the edge of the forest. I knew perfectly well what it was hiding. The summer brought boletes there, and the autumn drew parasol mushrooms out of the soil. The mushroom spawn was bulging in that spot: widespread, fertile, producing abundant fruit. All right, Grandpa replied at the time. It'll be yours.

We're watching the strangers here.

There are white houses rising on the plot promised to me.

They've already put up fences, I say.

Yes, says Ann.

They've dug up the mushroom spawn, I say.

The concrete mixers are turning, turning, turning.

SCAR

Did it heal nicely, er, that scar of yours? asks Staszek.

I feel as if he's asking someone who's standing next to me, as if it cannot be true that he's aiming the question at me. What on earth can he know about the fire that melted my groin? The secret of my childhood pain belongs to this house, doesn't it? I think, in a fever that floods my face.

He's watching.

I'm watching.

I'm asking you if it healed up, er, that scar of yours? he repeats.

Oh, you insolent prick, I think of him and mentally add: Yes, fuck you, it did, do you want to know if there's pubic hair growing on that scar of mine, or what? Is that the sort of detail you want? I scream internally, but from my own lips I hear: Yes, thank you, it all healed up nicely.

I was there – do you remember? he goes on.

He must know that I can't remember.

You were brought out of the stable unconscious, he says. They told me to, er, look after your mouth, I mean your head.

I took it in my hands and held it. Well, so you wouldn't choke on nothing, while your grandpa and grandma, er, fumbled around down there, getting your clothes off, you had a skirt, a green one, some sort of polyester, it must have been artificial, 'cos it was all sort of melded into you. Your grandma kept pouring water over your body. Your grandpa covered your legs with thighs fetched out of the freezer, turkey thighs I think. There were lots of them. But that's probably not what you do for burns. We all went a bit crazy at the time. Yes. While you were unconscious, it didn't seem all that bad, but when you came round, pardon me, but the world went fucking apeshit. All hell broke loose. You screamed, you snarled and lost consciousness again. You were like an animal. The way it looked to me, you were knocked out by the pain. I didn't come by for a whole week, 'cos I was scared of your screaming, it was like a razor blade.

Why didn't you people take me to the hospital? I ask.

I can't remember, he says, there could have been plum brandy in our systems, er, in our veins, in our heads. Yes. That was it. Do you, er, remember any of it?

I don't remember you, I say, but I do remember the fire that splashed me here – I point at my groin area and immediately regret the gesture – and then cold and fire, cold and fire. Hell.

Hell, yeah, he mumbles.

Ah! And I also remember, I go on, Grandpa giving me a hundred zlotys to stop screaming, so I took the money and squeezed it in my hand, but I went on screaming. Then he said he'd give me all the beehives, he said they were mine, and that now, from now on – if I stopped bawling my head off, of course, that's what he said – he'd work for me in what was now my apiary. We exchanged glances, Grandpa must have seen that I scorned his offer, because then he said the pigeons were mine too. We came to an agreement. I shut my gob, and then I screamed a different way, to the inside, deep down.

Yeah, yeah, he says.

Ann appears.

Nobody says a word.

In her presence Staszek loses his voice.

He stares after her, following every bit of her, every movement.

That night Ann says: That man is wild.

Yes, I say.

PORK LOIN

At last, says Grandpa, handing me a Klub. We're on the veranda, watching the plumbers' van from Stary Sad. At dawn Grandpa wiped the dust off the radiator ribs that many months ago they helped him to stack in the hall. In a few days from now they'll be heating the body of the house.

High time, says Grandpa.

For three days we and Grandma move from room to room, sleeping wherever the walls aren't being disturbed by the men. Every blow they strike at the walls seems to ring in our heads. There are migraines rising in our frontal lobes. The only warm spot in the house is by the kitchen stove. We cover Grandma in a layer of hot-water bottles.

Now and then I spy on the men. They know how to do their job. They leave no trace of themselves behind. Wall after wall, a complicated constellation of pipes grows in the house as the long radiator ribs are installed under the windows.

Ann is cooking for everyone.

This is disgusting, she says as she picks up the fresh pork loin brought by Staszek. She tenderizes the meat with a mallet, dips it in beaten egg, then into breadcrumbs, and immerses it in heated fat. The men like the lunch.

Meat, says one of them and chews it at length, closing his eyes as if it afforded him bliss.

Ann serves them compote. I look at her hands. They're red. I know where that's from. She had to scrub them for ages with a metal scourer.

CITRUS

February has brought snow. First Grandpa feeds the deep bellies of our cows, a little later he feeds the great belly of the central furnace, and through it he feeds the now instated radiator ribs.

The stable is part of this house. As a child I thought all houses were home to both people and animals, and that everywhere you went downstairs through a cupboard into the stable. It was years before I discovered that our house is the only one like it in this valley.

Whence the idea of living above the animals, of the house rising from the stable? I ask Grandpa at daybreak as we're mucking out together.

You need to be able to hear the animals, he says.

We live above the animals. Over the past few decades the whole house has become imbued with the smell of horses, cows, pigs, hens and turkeys.

It's the first thing I sense, that smell, said Ann, when in a cloud of citrus perfume she entered the house after her long journey.

I'm made of that smell, I tell her, I can recognize that smell anywhere and I can be recognized by it.

BEECH

I walk across the stable to join Grandpa in the cellar. It's there, in a space beside the animals, that room has been made for the furnace. This boiler room is clean and large. Grandpa can't hear me. My footsteps blend with the groaning of the animals, the creaking of the beams beneath their feet and the sound of their pissing. I find him staring into the fire. The furnace door is not shut. I go closer. His face is bathed in warmth, it's absorbing it.

He's talking to the furnace.

Find out where the heat's escaping, he says.

Lots and lots has been wasted, he says.

The time is coming, we must arm ourselves with wood, with honey, he says.

Let the cows be fat, he says.

We must take the cat to the city, have it all cut off, there are gingers all over May, he says.

Steel, steel, he says.

He notices me.

This house has never had such warmth before, he says, addressing me now.

Yes, I say.

We'll have to swap Grandma's eiderdown for a summer quilt. Any moment she'll go up in flames, he says.

Yes, I say.

He closes the little door, touches the metal of the furnace and straightens his back.

Come on, he says.

I go after him. I can see him examining the entire architecture of the central heating, he knows where the pipes are going, he's following their routes, although they're hidden in the walls. He stops by each radiator, checks the setting and turns it on full. He does it throughout the house.

In Grandma's room the men from Stary Sad have installed long radiator ribs under each of the windows.

Grandpa goes up to them, feels them and says: Hot.

I take off my sweater.

It's boiling in the house.

Sultry.

I think of the forest that will be fodder for our furnace, I think of the beech trees that I'll help Grandpa to carry down into the valley, about the ones in the topmost fields, I think about the birch tree and its papery skin that kindles fire under everything. I think about how greedy the house is. This house was always chilly, there was always an icy nip in here. But now Grandpa has fitted it with radiator ribs and there's a heatwave here, there's no shelter from the warmth that sedates, slackens and deceives the body.

DOWRY

Nothing here belongs to me, says Grandma.

Everything belongs to you, I say. The plants belong to you, the walnut tree growing behind the house belongs to you, the rosary from Medjugorje belongs to you. Lots of thing here are yours: clothes, cosmetics, the picture of Our Lady of Fatima hanging on the wall, lots of things, I say, and nothing else comes to my mind.

She does, says Ann, pointing at me, she belongs to you.

Yes, I say.

I came to this house many years ago, says Grandma. I prayed to be found useful, to be a source of children. All I brought with me was a dog, a German shepherd, I called him Krat. That was the only thing I brought into this house. Just the dog, that was the dowry with which Grandpa accepted me. But he had a house, lots of forests and lots of fields, an apiary, an orchard. He gave me a surname. I was able to work hard, and also, thank God, I was able to give birth. Though the first thing I bore died, but it was alive for a while. Later there was your aunt, and your mother, twin sisters, there were two. He liked that. The doubling, he saw it as a sign. I have remained. But nothing here belongs to me. None of it is mine, I won't leave any things behind, there won't be any inheritance when I'm gone, no forced share. A few clothes will remain, yes, and you will remain – here Grandma points at me. You're able to work hard yourself and you should be able to bring live things into the world. You have broad hips. Maybe that will belong to me too, that will be from me, whatever you bring into the world.

But there's so much that's dead inside me, I'm thinking, though what I say is: Yes, yes.

KRAT

I've learnt to recognize the way he knocks. He's obstinate in his knocking. He's carrying something, he wants to present a gift, so it's right to open the door for him. I open it.

Pork knuckle for Róża, he says.

Thank you, I say.

The meat stinks. I'll feed it to the dog. I won't tell Grandma he was here again, I think.

He's standing in the doorway.

He's looking.

Thank you, I repeat.

I'd like to buy some honey.

Grandpa's not here.

I know, he says.

He's looking.

I'm looking.

Come in, I say.

He comes in. He takes off his bloodstained rubber boots. His socks are wet, they leave marks on the tiles with which the men from Stary Sad replaced the floorboards. He sits down on a stool by the window, between the table and the fridge. He spreads his legs. One thigh far from the other. He takes up space. He makes himself at home.

Tea? I ask.

Yes, he replies.

I have to bring it, he says after a pause.

I'm looking at him.

Go on, I say.

Flesh for flesh. It was my fault, that dog, that dog of your grandma's, that long-haired Alsatian, I don't know if she told you.

Never in detail, I say, I know from you that you have penance to do, nothing beyond that.

It was eight springs ago, he says. You were out of the country, they told me at the time, you weren't here much. I know, because I looked out for you. Róża had taken in the dog, a stray, injured by a car perhaps, or by a person. She cared for that dog. Sometimes I'd toss him something on the quiet, for some reason she didn't want meat from the slaughterhouse. And then the spring came. They put up posters about rabies on the telegraph poles, with a date and a location marked on them. The inoculation was going to take place here, outside the slaughterhouse. So on the day the whole valley gathered here. People brought their dogs down from the ridge and from the forest. Some had them on cow chains, some on pieces of cord, some on twine, several were running free. Those dogs had cuts on their napes and throats. They were growling at one another, nipping each other, but we were keeping a tight hold on them, each man held on to his own. They let me out of the slaughterhouse with those three pit bulls, I had them all on short ropes. Bloody brutes, not dogs, black devils. They didn't even have names, because at the slaughterhouse we didn't want any memory of them to remain. They were kept behind bars. The point was for them to be there, for them to bark occasionally, nothing more. The noise was needed, but it was more about the look of them, their job was to frighten. Just before the vet appeared, Róża came down from the house, here, across the meadow, with her rescued dog. Why did your grandpa let her out alone? There were no females there, but here she was with this clean, well-fed animal. She stood to one side and waited. Something sparked in my dogs, I don't know which one it was. Or how all three of them didn't break loose. I was holding them in a single fist, but they pulled so hard that bloody bastard strength of theirs twisted my arm.

Look, he says, showing me.

I look and see a misshapen wrist.

They went for Róża's dog. And they started to get in a spin, the bloody brutes. They dived under the bus I'd left outside the shop that morning to avoid cluttering the slaughterhouse yard. And there they started biting each other. They were hissing, it was like hell in there. Zbyszek, the blacksmith, shouted at me to move the vehicle. I jumped in the cab and moved off. Something raised such a howl beneath the wheels that it got into my bloodstream, and it's still ringing in my ears. I drove a few metres and left two bodies behind me. Your grandma's dog and one of our devils. Róża was watching, she went up to the dogs and screamed. I don't know what she screamed, because it wasn't human. But I know she was screaming at me, into me. And it was like a curse. It sits inside me. The dogs were pegging out. Their eyes were still moving, but their guts were on the outside. Róża came up to me and said: Finish him off. I did. And she took her dog's body, Krat was his name, I think, 'cos apparently long ago your grandma had had a similar dog and had passed the name on to this one. She slung him around her neck, the way sheep are carried in the holy pictures. And it was trickling down her, that dog's blood, two dogs' blood, because our devil's blood was mixed in too, so it was trickling down her. The dog's head was knocking against her ribcage. And that's how she went home. I'd never seen anyone love an animal like that, perhaps it's a sin to love it in a human way, but it's not for me to judge. I killed, and now I'm doing penance. And I laid the penance on myself. Flesh for flesh. Although your grandma has been telling me not to bring it from the start. I have to bring it. She put a curse on me then.

Would you like her to lift it? I ask.

No, he replies, no.

MIST

Tell me about the animals of this place, asks Ann.

I can see that her gaze is following the light cast by the glass face of the broken watch I wear on my wrist. I inherited it from my father, but time stopped in it at the moment of his passing. Ann is joined by Azrael, and together they follow the light, they study the light and try to catch it. I'm staring at their tensed muscles, tiny movements and vigilance. After a while I cover the watch face so Ann will be interested in my story again. It takes her quite a time to return to reality. She still has the spark reflected in her eyes.

She's glittering.

She's bright and beautiful.

The cat is licking Ann's skin.

At least tell me about one of the wild animals of this place, she says, refining her request.

All right, I say. I have a story for you about one of the animals, one that rises from the dead in the cold and damp, and perishes in the wind and sunshine. It's the only local animal

I haven't given a name. It doesn't need a name. It assumes various shapes, it weighs nothing. It always emerges from one single spot. Years ago I spied out where it was seeping from. There's this cave on the south bank of the stream. That's where it emerges from.

You call the mist an animal? asks Ann.

Yes. It has a muzzle. When you look at the body of the mist from the other side of the hill, you can see that just above our house it opens its muzzle and takes the house into itself. Sometimes, when I realize it's moving straight onto us, I open the windows and let it come inside the house. Then it gets damp in here. What remains of the mist moves onwards, to the ridge, and drops into the reservoir.

MIRRORS

I spot Grandpa on the roof of his shed. Since Ann arrived he's been padlocking it. He's been taking something down there at night, putting something aside, collecting something.

And now, as I can clearly see, he's pulling a few of the brick tiles off the roof and putting small panes of glass in their place.

He's letting in the light, I think.

I tell Ann about it.

For a while she's pensive, as if considering whether to tell me something she knows about or keep it to herself.

One time I suspected what he has in there, she says at last. It's a vast burial ground. A cemetery for mirrors. There are lots of them in there. They're the saddest mirrors in the world. They have no access to anything bright. It's against their nature. Mirrors like that aren't alive, they don't multiply anything.

A burial ground for mirrors? I ask.

Yes, she says, and continues: Now brightness will get in there through those holes in the roof and they'll start reflecting into infinity.

I try to imagine it: a mirror reflects a mirror, which reflects a reflection, which reflects the reflection of the reflection, and there's no end of it in sight.

TRANSYLVANIA

I recognize his knock.

I open the door.

Good day, I say.

I look.

Now I know, he starts, I should have been bringing live things to this house, and I stupidly brought death.

You don't have to bring anything to this house, I say.

I must, he replies.

He hands me a shopping bag in which something is moving and squeaking. I peep inside and see four chicks, thickly coated in fluff, but naked around their necks, as if they've been shaved.

What's this? I ask.

At the market they said it's a breed from distant Romania, from Transylvania, immune to illness, no plague can catch them, no fever or other pestilence. And they say it has tasty meat, and the hens can lay lots of big eggs each month. The saleswoman said they're, the eggs, are a red colour, and not to be scared of that, it's just their look.

What am I to do with them? I ask.

Feed them, he says.

Thank you, I reply and close the door. Through the opaque glass panel I can see him standing in front of it for ages, as if waiting for me to open it again. Once he has gone away, I take the living things to Grandma.

Look, I say, and fetch out the chicks.

Grandma looks.

Grotesque, she says.

As if hawks had plucked their necks, says Ann, who puts down her book and examines the live things.

Give them here, says Grandma, pointing at the quilt. The chicks run around the cobalt-blue duvet cover, soon find a dip in the softness, just at the height of Grandma's hips, and flock together into a single organism. Grandma holds out a hand to them, closes her eyes and blindly seeks the naked necks of the Transylvanian fowl. Stroking involves only one of her fingers, the index finger on her right hand. There's no strength for more in her.

I watch.

After a few minutes everything that's alive on the bed sinks into sleep.

LOVE

Grandma's illness has lasted for a million years, I say to Ann.
Yes, may it last a million years, she says.

PHEASANT

The house's illness and Grandma's illness have driven me out into the landscape. I'm suffocating in this house, I say to myself aloud. I like this timbre, finally it can be mine, authentic.

I say and hear myself: I hate the walls of this house; I hate the stink, the shit, the blood that comes from the slaughterhouse; I hate the frost that paints flowers on the windows of the stable; I hate my hands, which stink of death; I hate Grandpa and his slow movements, his Klub cigarettes; I hate Ann and her calm, her beauty, her fragrance, her body, the way she watches; I hate Grandma and the fact that she's nurturing something inside her, I hate the fact that she's alive, and the fact that she's dying.

I take a deep breath, and as I breathe out I swear into the snow-covered topmost fields on the ridge.

I manage to startle a pheasant. It runs out of a birch grove and stops in the middle of the field. It stands there. I stand there too. We look at each other. Then it emits a sound that cuts the air in two. It manages to jostle everything that's fragile inside me.

Shortly after it goes off into the forest. I sit down in the snow on the ridge in the spot where the fields drop steeply, some towards May, and the rest towards the reservoir created years ago on top of Grandma's village.

I put snow into my mouth.

I'm eating snow.

A fox runs along the edge of the forest, picks up the trail of a bird, and comes to a stop in the middle of the field. Earlier lots of wild things must have roamed this way. The fox sits down in the snow. I narrow my eyes. It looks as if a bonfire were burning in the white field. It's coming up. My head is spinning. I lie down in the snow. Above my muzzle I can see the fox's muzzle.

Fire, I think.

The fox is coming closer.

I'm licked by a tongue of fire.

I'm set alight by fire.

Brightness closes my eyes.

RIDGE

Drink, says Ann, shoving a thermos under my nose.

Wild rosehip tea burns my tongue.

We're all sick here, she starts, everyone.

I realize I'm in the snow, on the topmost ridge. I can't feel my body.

I look at Ann. She's beautiful. She smells of salvia.

I came here by following your footprints, I saw others along the way, but only yours were trailing, because you even walk in a way that shows you're sick, stricken with something. We're all sick in this house, do you know that? It'd be simplest to leave, not to give a shit, she says, raising her voice. But I can't. I'm sick in this too, I share it with the rest of you. I want you to know that when I saw you lying here in the snow, with a fox beside you that, look, trod out a hollow around you, but raced into the forest at the sight of me, I thought you were betraying me, that you were leaving me. You bitch, I thought. But I realize it wasn't like that, and I take it back, she says.

She strokes my eyebrows.

I look at her and I know I was sinking into a fatal sleep.

In this house, you, she continues, are the sickest of us all, it's you.

REFLECTION

I've got something for you, Grandpa says to Ann.

What's the occasion? she asks.

A bright day, let that suffice, he replies and pushes a rusted little key across the oilcloth.

A bright day, so be it, she says. Where to?

To the shed, we hear.

Ann glances at me.

I've heard that for the past few years you've been studying the light, says Grandpa. I don't understand much of it. I know you're working on a doctorate about light. The title 'doctor' means a lot here in the valley. And a female doctor means even more. I thought I'd prepare you a place where you can conduct your research. There's plenty to study here. It may even be better to study the light here than in those Asian temples of yours. Ever since you've been here, I've seen how you look at the mirrors, how you study the way the sunbeams fall. Grey days make you quiet, don't they? I can see how you seek the sunbeams and stand in them. You know all about reflections.

And in the west room you've arranged the light by the mirrors for Grandma so she looks healthier in them, fuller. I profit from it too. You know how to dig around in artificial light. Going into Grandma's room is like going into life, not death. And it occurred to me that perhaps you need a place where you'll be able to dig around by the light of day.

Can we go and see? asks Ann.

Grandpa nods.

Ann turns the key. The padlock gives way. We go inside. There's light falling in through the panes of glass in the roof. All the walls are festooned in mirrors. Grandpa must have been collecting them in the village, he must have brought a lot of them from the marketplace in Stary Sad. I can see hundreds of Ann's face and hundreds of Grandpa's face, and hundreds of myself. We can see that Grandpa was interested in the mirrors that were damaged, had a crack in them. That's why whichever mirror I look into, not only is the reflection multiplied, there's a flaw in it too.

Thank you, says Ann and goes up to one of the mirrors. It's composed of many pieces. Ann lays a hand on it and runs it over the glass. A streak of blood from her finger is left on it.

There's lots to study in there, says Ann that night.

CLOSE-UP

Ann makes use of the mirror shed. She disappears in there on days when the sun is beating down on the valley. With Grandpa's help she has swapped several more roof tiles for panes of glass. After many months Ann is back to making notes again.

I've got my own laboratory, she says, it's a pity not to use it.

Every time I go in, I find her in a different spot, notebook in hand. Words land on the pages, and sketches too. It all resembles the kanji characters that have fascinated Ann for years. At night she more and more often keeps me company in the room in the attic, from where I connect with the world and devise pure code, but also poems of course. Our bodies are illuminated by artificial light. We rattle away at our keyboards: tap, tap, tap, tap, tap.

Grandpa hasn't stopped collecting mirrors. Today he brought home the door of an old wardrobe that the parish chairwoman threw out. I recognize it. He found it taken to pieces by the main road just before a vehicle arrived marked 'large bulky items'.

There's no room in the shed for any more mirrors. That doesn't stop Grandpa. He fixes the wardrobe door and its mirror onto the shed door, so now, before you go inside this kingdom of mirrors, you have to look at yourself from head to foot. The mirror has an interesting property that we like – everything that faces it becomes narrow.

The mirrors drive me mad, I say to Ann many days later.

Why's that? she asks.

Because they multiply me. Wherever I turn, I'm visible, and there, in the shed, I'm visible from every side. And I become aware that I exist spatially in three dimensions, and that's unbearable, I add. But they also tempt me, I say.

Shhh, go to sleep, says Ann.

GINGER

The mirrors tempt me. At times when Ann is busy with other matters, I sneak into the shed and look. I'm duplicated. I stand in one spot. Only my eyes are working away, but after that I set my head in motion, my arms, hands, legs.

The light is warm and it slides across my body. It occurs to me to touch myself.

And I touch myself.

And everything in this interior is moving. And I see myself multiplied. Lots of hands are making moves towards my body. I'm not ashamed of anything. I'm putting myself on display, the mirrors can see me, but no one alive can see me, I'm thinking. I don't shout. I don't raise my voice. In this family every caress happens in silence. The noise remains inside me and radiates on the inside where it quivers, quivers.

As the noise quivers inside me here, at the same time other noises are lingering in the village: the postwoman is scouring her parka pocket with her fingers in search of a five-zloty coin to pay the father of the Swarts the tail end of the rent, though she knows the coin will come back to her as a tip; the parish chairwoman is grating ginger on the grater's smallest slots; inside Malina the hay she's eaten is turning over; Ann is using a knife to rip the plastic wrapping, takes out a handful of clay pebbles and then fills the bottom of a flowerpot with them; the bee mother raises a limb and then lowers it; at the slaughterhouse someone hurls a swearword, followed by peals of the workmen's laughter; a demijohn set up in the warm bathroom with wild cherry wine maturing inside it releases an air bubble, which emerges through a glass pipe – pop; Grandma scratches herself on her white belly; the nasal bone of a boy from Stary Sad who walked into May as if entering his own home breaks; the wind and rain are gathering strength – they're licking the roof and the glass panes; Staszek swallows saliva and crunches a snail shell under his boot, I can hear it just past one of the shed planks.

THURSDAY

Only when Ann is close can I find my bearings in time. Ann keeps an eye on time. She knows. Whenever she leaves the house, we get completely confused, Grandma and I, above all we confuse time, and as a result when to take meals, when to take medicine, the number of naps that we can't suppress, but we don't know how long they last, because what's outside the window doesn't tell us if it's morning or early evening. Like today, when Grandma and I are woken by Grandpa.

It's halfway through the day, he says.

I get up and feed us medicine. Two pills for me. Four pills for Grandma. I take off the old morphine patch and stick on a new one. We don't eat anything because it doesn't occur to us.

We go to bed.

We're woken by the noise of pigs from the slaughterhouse.

I wake up as if it were a new day.

Is it a new day? asks Grandma.

Yes, I say.

What about the rooster, did he crow? she asks.

Donchiquito? Hmm, I didn't hear him, I reply.

I get up and feed us medicine. Two pills for me. Four pills for Grandma. Grandma presents her other side and I'm surprised there's no morphine patch on it, I stick on a new one. We don't eat anything because it doesn't occur to us.

Where the hell is Ann? I think.

We drop off to sleep.

We're woken by Ann, who's back from Stary Sad, with new pyjamas for Grandma and marigold face cream for me.

Have you been asleep the whole time? she asks.

It occurs to me that now it's the next day.

Yes, I tell her.

She looks and watches my movements.

I get up and feed us medicine. Two pills for me. Four pills for Grandma. I ask Ann to stick on Grandma's morphine patch. Ann pulls off Grandma's shirt.

There are two fresh patches here, she says.

What's the day today? asks Grandma.

Still the same as this morning, when I went off to town, says Ann, now it's early evening.

According to us it should be Thursday by now, I say.

No, says Ann.

I look at the pill blisters. I think about the megadoses of medicine that are now inside me, I look at Grandma and think about what's flowing in her veins right now.

I feel weak, I say.

So do I, says Grandma.

We go to bed.

Everything here is sick, I think, moments before falling asleep yet again that day.

TICK-TOCK

You died, but you came to life, you were lost, but you are found, says Grandma between spoonfuls of pigeon broth that I'm guiding to her narrow lips.

I was driven away from here by the death of my parents and aunt, I think, and I've been brought back by the next death to be hanging over this house. Everything here ticks: tick-tock, tick-tock, tick-tock, tick-tock, to a point of loss.

I'm shaken out of my reverie by a noise coming from Grandma's belly. Something's overflowing in her guts. Exactly the way it overflows in the guts of this house – it occurs to me – whenever Grandpa feeds the furnace and hot water moves into the pipes to heat the boiler and then the radiator ribs.

You were lost, but you are found, she carries on, louder, as if wanting to deafen the noises coming from her body, which as I can see are embarrassing her. You were lost, but you are found and now you are all my daughters at once and you carry in you all my grandsons and granddaughters. And there's lots and lots to be born from me.

SIROCCO

A funeral ceremony. Modest gestures, the coarse texture of the parish chairwoman's jacket. The slender bodies of the people from the Baltic coast. The wind works away in the faded red of Grandma's dress hanging on the wild cherry in the orchard. The spirit of the orchard.

Cows can be heard mooing. Our cows are mooing at the slaughterhouse. Rybowicz's cow along with them. Grandpa took them there a week ago. It's all for Grandma, he said the next morning, but the radiator ribs were already heating the house.

They weren't just yours, I screamed at him the one and only time in my life, right then.

It's all for Grandma, for you, for all of you, he said.

And now there's wind, warm and dusty.

The sirocco of these hills and this valley, I think.

People are emerging from every house to join the funeral procession.

They're curious, I say to Ann.

Yes, they are, she says.

I'm thinking about life, about lighting a cigarette and about someone touching me, but not in mourning, not as the granddaughter of the dead man. I want somebody's hands, her hands – I'm looking at the postwoman in the crowd; his hands – I'm looking at the Swart, who told me that time, many years ago, up there in the tree, that there was a lot to lick up in me; I want all the hands here present to touch me at once and caress me.

Mourning is voracious, I think.

Danube and Azrael are running across the fields towards the cortège. First they take their places at the back of the procession. Soon they get lost in the crowd, and only now and then do I see their bodies flashing by among the black clothes.

Ann nudges me and points to the right, towards the school we're passing. From there a white goose is waddling in our direction.

Could a poem come out of this? asks Ann.

Could it? I ask myself.

A MILLION YEARS

In the west room with Grandma, who has been dying for a million years and will go on dying for just as long, Staszek has stayed behind. Only later will we learn that he has wrung the necks of two of the Transylvanian chickens, because he couldn't find any more pigeons. He did it to make Grandma a nourishing feast for Grandpa's funeral.

Coming back from the cemetery I see Azrael on a manure heap outside the house, playing with a rooster's head. He's patting the red comb with his paws.

He's enjoying that, I think.

SLEEP

Grandma can't fall asleep without the noise of the table saw. So when no one in the village is playing their machine, I stand over the circular blade and under its teeth I place some thick greengage branches made ready by Grandpa.

REMEDY

In the attic I find cleansed dandelion roots. The remedy for death. Grandpa made supplies of it to last for years. I'm walking between the antlers hanging from the beams. Soon all this will have to be taken out of here. The men from Stary Sad want to set about replacing the roof.

Grandpa, I think, you didn't leave any orders, instructions or pointers.

But maybe he did?

Give back the wild to the wild?

SKY

For months the illness has been waving Grandma's hands towards the sky. The spring has chased away the cold. Dampness has set in. In this weather the voices of the missel thrushes sound as if passed through a sheet of water, they're more like the echo of their song than the actual thing.

When Grandma wakes, with the finger joints of her right hand, the one closer to the radiator, she plays softly on the cool ribs of this house: tap, tap, tap, tap, tap, tap.

Acknowledgements

For your inspiration, thank you to everything that's wild.

Thank you to my first readers, Justyn and Wit. Beautiful are the beings that fortify other beings, I'm thinking.

Thank you to my dear Rafał and my wonderful editor Dorota for accompanying this book. Your support remains with me.

Sources

Yes, to be one with the night: Gunnar Ekelöf, *Songs of Something Else: Selected Poems*, translated by Leonard Nathan and James Larson, Princeton University Press, Princeton, 1982, pp. 75 and 77.

The agave lives three hundred years: Krystyna Miłobędzka, *Spis z natury / Anaglify* ('List from nature / Anaglyphs'), Wydawnictwo Wolno, Lusowo, 2019, p. 36. (Quotation translated by Antonia Lloyd-Jones.)

Faithful creatures hacked to death: Tadeusz Nowak, 'Psalm wigilijny' ('Christmas Eve Psalm') in *Psalmy wszystkie* ('All the Psalms'), Państwowy Instytut Wydawniczy, Warsaw, 1980, p. 13. (Quotation translated by Antonia Lloyd-Jones.)

Riding birds, feeling under our thighs the soft feathers: Czesław Miłosz, 'Earth', from *The Garden of Earthly Delights*, translated by Czesław Miłosz and Robert Hass, *New and Collected Poems 1931–2001*, Allen Lane, London, 2001, p. 405.

The quoted descriptions of birds are from the *Collins Bird Guide*, text and maps by Lars Svensson, plates and captions by Killian Mullarney and Dan Zetterström, translated by David Christie, HarperCollins, London, 1999.

Translator's Afterword

This story is set in a village in the Beskid Sądecki mountain range, which lies to the south-east of Kraków, close to the Slovak border. At this point the landscape consists of steep hills and deep valleys, the prelude to higher mountains. The fictional village of May is typical of these parts: a road running through the valley, parallel to a stream, with houses scattered along it and up the hillslopes on either side; here the inevitable landmarks are the shop, the school, the church, the cemetery and the slaughterhouse. These locations are not just on the village map, but on the map of life – everything happens around them. Life follows some simple, immutable patterns, the same for centuries, and death is never far away. But equally life never ceases to fight back, hold out and renew itself.

Before starting work on this translation, I felt a need to go to the region and absorb its atmosphere. I was hoping to get a sense of the omnipresence of both life and death, as described in this book, and the precarious balance between them that has a constant bearing on human existence. I wasn't disappointed.

It's a beautiful, wild place that makes you aware that you're just another tiny part of nature. Up on the hilltop, the view reminds you of eternity: ridge upon ridge like waves, stretching away to the horizon. The fields and the forest are seething with life, birds call among the trees, insects swarm in the grass that's thick with wild flowers and herbs, the trees are laden with fruit and berries, everything grows abundantly and the night sky is bright with stars. Everything's alive, and your senses are fully engaged – sight, hearing, smell and touch. But I also saw cows penned in a small, muddy enclosure, animals born only to die and be butchered.

Małgorzata Lebda's language has been shaped by this landscape. Known chiefly as a poet, this is her first venture into prose, and it stems directly from her poetry, in terms of both themes and style. To me this text is a whole, not a linear narrative but a carefully woven series of lyric images, full of echoes and rhythms. The influence of Church language is palpable; in a village like May the Bible is the only literary work familiar to all the parishioners and prayers and hymns are the best-known songs, and we can hear that influence in Lebda's cadences and vocabulary. But nature is even more powerful than God; the narrator has broken away from the Church and identifies with the fox. Here people are on a par with everything else in nature: cows, horses, pigs, dogs, cats, insects and plants. Everything is animate or personified, even the stream, the earth, the trees, the house, bones, and of course the illness. Sensory words echo throughout the text, sights, smells, sounds, the damp, the cold, the heat; colours abound: white, pink, green; light and dark are constantly contrasted; and the equilibrium between life and death is recalibrated again and again.

As translator of this exquisite text, I felt as if I needed to be inside an egg, a white cocoon with no angles, so that nothing could distract me from the purity of the text while I was working on it. But life is full of interruptions and no such luxury exists. To my surprise, I found it easy to go in and out of Lebda's world and to feel comfortable inside it every time. I was conscious throughout of the need to retain the poetry of the original, which relies on sparseness, rhythms, repetitions, silences and precision. As an inflected language, Polish is much better suited to terseness than English, but I've tried to retain the concision, because the number of syllables, and therefore the rhythm, contributes to the effect the words are having on the reader, whether they're conscious of it or not. Repetitions are tricky too, because in translation the same word doesn't always work well in every instance, but I have done my best to retain the echoes within the text. Sometimes it was hard to choose tenses, because Polish has few of them, English many; for instance, when the narrator thinks rather than says something, 'I think' is sometimes better served by 'I'm thinking', or by putting 'I think to myself'. There are no inverted commas for speech in this book, just inserted phrases such as 'I say', 'he asks', etc., a feature I have retained because the apparent simplicity of the text adds to its atmosphere. As I read it, there's also a lot of silence in the book, which I believe to be part of the narrative.

Some aspects of the story are deliberately left unexplained; for instance, who is Ann? Is she the narrator's sister? Cousin? Lover? Or just a friend? We never discover her exact relationship to this family, but I think of her as the mirror image of the narrator, her reflection, the light that contrasts with the narrator's darkness; Ann tends towards life, while the narrator tends towards death – it is Ann who rescues her in her near-fatal moment of despair.

Translating is a personal experience. As a translator I feel I must let the original text into my bloodstream, allowing it to affect me emotionally, or else I won't fully understand the writer's intentions. In this particular case I can only start to imagine what courage it took to write this book, and to express such a raw experience in such a beautiful, poetic way. I hope my translation does justice to the power of Lebda's sensitive and poignant writing.

Founded in 2023, Linden Editions is dedicated to publishing outstanding literary works of fiction, narrative non-fiction, reportage and essays. These are primarily in translation, from Europe, the Francophonie and the Mediterranean region.

We live and work internationally and enjoy a mixture of cultures, identities and traditions. We intend to use this access to world literature to discover books that merit international exposure: books which tell compelling stories; books which bring fresh, unforgettable voices; and books which are committed, urgent and challenging.

Linden trees grow all over the world, and are often planted at the centre of village squares. People have been gathering under their shade for generations to share stories. Many cultures see the linden tree as sacred, its perfume all-pervading, and its tea curative. Just like the seeds spread by linden trees, we hope our books will spread the seeds of internationalism further.

To discover more, visit lindeneditions.com.

OUR TITLES IN 2025

Voracious · Małgorzata Lebda
translated from the Polish by Antonia Lloyd-Jones

In Late Summer · Magdalena Blažević
translated from the Croatian by Anđelka Raguž

I folgorati · Susanna Bissoli
translated from the Italian by Georgia Wall

Corps de ferme · Agnès de Clairville
translated from the French by Frank Wynne

Not There · Mariusz Szczygieł
translated from the Polish by Antonia Lloyd-Jones